.Cesario.

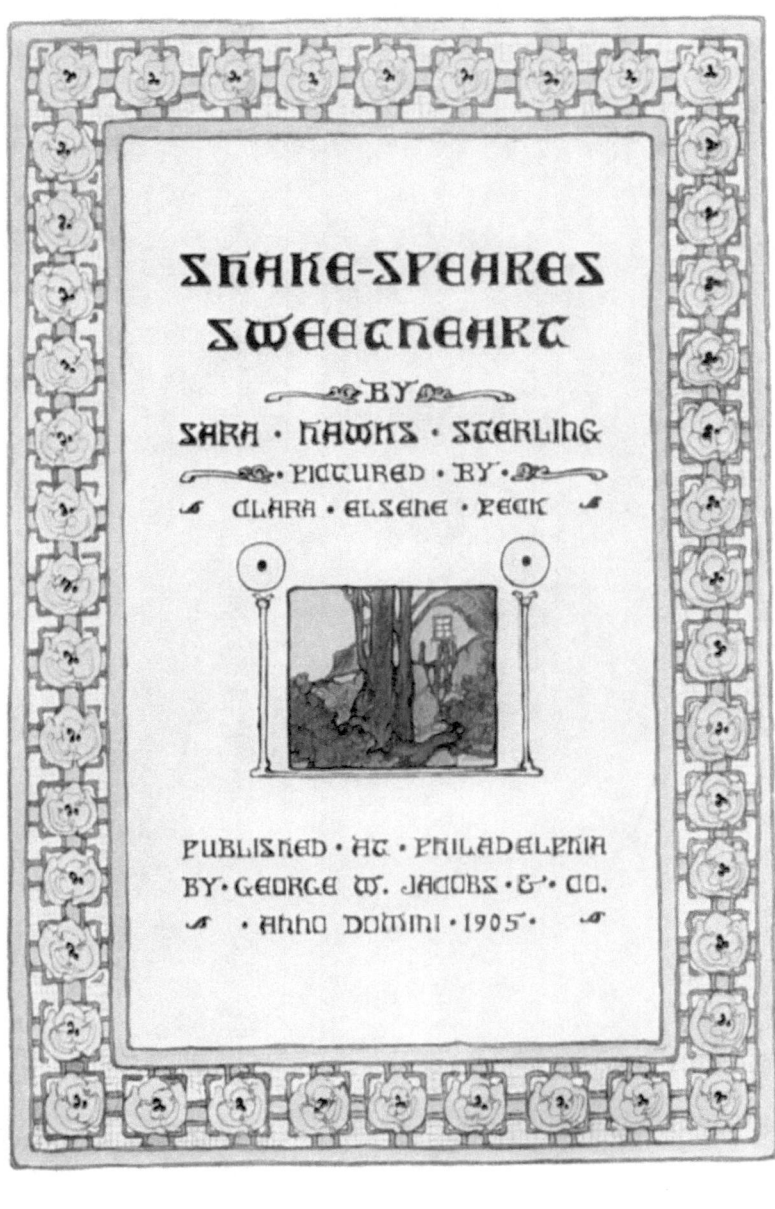

SHAKE-SPEARES SWEETHEART

BY

SARA · HAWKS · STERLING

· PICTURED · BY ·

CLARA · ELSENE · PECK

PUBLISHED · AT · PHILADELPHIA
BY · GEORGE W. JACOBS · & · CO.
· ANNO DOMINI · 1905 ·

To My Mother

Contents

Illustrations

Chapter I

How Master Jon-son Came to Stratford

Five years have now passed since he left us—and the world that will forever love and mourn him. Five times have the seasons run their course since he fell asleep beside the Avon, never to waken more. Five long and lonely years! And yet—and yet—to me it seems that he is never far away. Lonely in body have I been, but never hath my soul dwelt solitary. My grief for him is as no other's; yet my joy is such as none can ever take from me. I was his, he was mine. The world's poet was my beloved, too. It makes me almost catch my breath to say it, and I often marvel why this crown of my life was given me. 'Tis a mystery sweet as strange, a very sacrament of wonder and of love. And a mystery, whether human or divine, we may adore, but never comprehend.

For I was Shakespeare's sweetheart—verily and alone his sweetheart, even after I became his wedded wife. From that first wondrous day when we read in

each other's eyes the new-born love which was to live forever, to the time when he left me for a while, five years ago; nay, even until now, I am Shakespeare's sweetheart. And so it is my right, as it is also my pride and delight, to tell the story of our love for the great multitudes who held Will dear, for the shadowy, unborn multitudes who shall pay homage to his memory in years to come. Truly, the story is sacred to me; but he is not mine alone; he is also the world's, the world that loved him, that he loved.

After all, however, Master Ben Jonson is responsible for my trying to tell this tale of mine. For yesterday, with a great noise and bustle, as is his wont, he rode up to the gates of New Place and called loudly for me. I was sitting in the garden, sewing, and the instant after he had bellowed forth my name he beheld me.

"Good-morrow, Mistress Shakespeare," he cried, waving his hand to me. "Thou art the very dame I wish to see. Art weary, art busy? If so, I will leave my errand until later. This sorry nag of mine must be stabled at the inn;" and he gave a vicious dig at the poor beast he bestrode. Master Jonson is not at his best on horseback.

14

"I am neither weary nor busy, Master Jonson," I replied, walking down to the gateway, that we might converse more freely. "Prythee, come in at once; Will's friends are always welcome at New Place."

"Marry, it is about Will that I would speak with thee," he said, bluntly, looking at me with shrewd, kindly eyes. "Moreover, I am mistaken sorely if my errand shall not please thee. Natheless, on my way hither I ordered dinner at the inn, and I must e'en go there first. Then I will return, an it like thee. I have many things to talk about."

I expressed my pleasure at the prospect, and he looked delighted. "I will return, then, as speedily as may be," he said, beginning a somewhat unsuccessful attempt to turn his horse about. "Au revoir, Mistress Shakespeare, and may all the gods of Olympus—— The devil take thee, thou evil-faced, sorry steed! Accursed be the day I hired thee! Wilt thou obey my rein? Ah, at last. Go on, thou imp of Satan!" With which cheerful adjuration Master Jonson ambled away, too absorbed in guiding his steed to take further notice of me then.

I laughed a little as I watched his ungraceful progress; but as I turned from the gate I sighed.

15

Master Jonson had been Will's true friend. They had loved each other right well. I remembered, on the day of Will's funeral, how swollen and marred with tears had been that kindly, whimsical face into which I had just been looking. What could it be in connection with Will that he had to say to me? No matter what, it would be something arising from the love these two had borne toward each other. So thinking, I once more seated myself in the garden, took up my sewing and awaited Master Jonson's return.

An hour later I saw him again approaching. He was on foot this time, and looked much more comfortable than before. I smiled and nodded to him, and rose to give him welcome. An instant after, we were seated at the table in our garden where, in years gone by, Will had often entertained his London friends. My little maid brought us cakes and wine, then left us. Master Jonson smacked his lips at sight of them.

"Mistress Shakespeare, thou good angel!" he cried. "Execrable was my inn dinner, but now thou wilt make amends. Well do I remember," and a shadow fell over his face, "well do I remember thy hospitality of yore."

I replied, simply, that I was glad he was pleased, and bade him do justice to the fare, since he approved

16

it. Nothing loth, he attacked the wine, and had drunk several glasses before he spoke again.

"Methinks Will was right," he said at length, suddenly; "he told me once that there was one woman who could guard her tongue," and he looked at me with a twinkle in his eyes. I smiled at his words, although a little sadly.

"Will said many things that I did not deserve," I replied; "nor do I think I have justified in my life the opinion thou hast quoted. I betrayed my one great secret in a moment of terror and distress. Natheless, 'tis sooth that I have never been prone to gossip after the fashion of my sex."

"Art anxious to know what hath brought me down thus suddenly from London?" he said, abruptly, pouring out more wine.

I answered, truthfully, that I was; but added that I would await his convenience to tell me his errand.

"And, therefore, one woman can restrain her natural curiosity," he replied, promptly and teasingly. "Will was right. Well, virtue shall be rewarded, and I will tell thee at once. Thou know'st Will's plays— Hamlet, Romeus and Juliet, Much Ado and the rest?"

I nodded, silently, my eyes fixed upon his face.

17

"And soothly," he continued, gazing at me thoughtfully, "I think I know now why the women of Will's plays are—what they are. The rest of us cannot picture women. We can show drabs or shrews, but Portias and Imogens are not for us. I know why now; there is but one Anne Hathaway."

I blushed at that, for it was base flattery. I am not a young woman now, and what girlish charm I may have had is gone.

"You cozen me, Master Jonson," I observed with some coldness; "you cozen me, indeed; and it is ill done of one whom Will deemed his dear friend. Surely you seek some favor of me that you give me these soft words."

"Nay," he said, eagerly, "nay, and yet ay. It is true I seek a favor; but, on my soul, I seek not to cozen thee. Let me tell thee without more words than need be. These plays of Will's—never had our London players such to perform, nor ever will again—are at last to be published. Art not pleasured by these tidings?"

I assented, but a little doubtfully. "I wonder——" I began.

"I know what thou wouldst say," interrupted

Master Jonson, quickly; "thou dost wonder whether Will's honor would permit this to be done, were he alive. Ay, Mistress Shakespeare, for I would not countenance the proceeding else. I love his honor as my own, nor would I see it smirched. The public seeks now to have these plays in print, and in a form put forth in authorized fashion. While Will lived it was different. He sought not a dishonorable double profit, after the fashion of some. Having sold his play to the theatre, he took it not also to the printer's. But now conditions are changed. Were Will himself alive, he would do what John Hemminge and John Condell seek to do for him—to prepare the plays for publication. Their work is one of love, but, of necessity, imperfect. Would that he were here to do it for himself! God knows I wish it sore!"

He dropped his face into his hands and was silent for an instant. As for me, sudden tears blinded me, and I sat gazing at the garden with eyes that beheld, as in a vision, the beloved form I could no longer see with mortal sight. For a moment we sat thus. Then, with an impetuous movement, Master Jonson raised his head, and, rapidly pouring out two glasses of wine, handed one to me.

"To his memory!" he cried, holding the other aloft. "To his memory, and to his soul's rest! Will Shakespeare, Comrade and Poet!"

We drank the little toast together.

"It is glad news, indeed, then," I said. "Since the act smircheth not his honor, I shall be right glad to see the plays in lawful printed form. Thou wilt superintend the task, Master Jonson?"

"Ay," he answered, flushing with delight at my pleased tone. There was always much of the child about him, despite his learning. "I am glad that thou approvest. Were't otherwise, the enterprise would end forthwith. Ay, I will see that as few errors are made as may be. Master Hemminge and Master Condell will perform their task faithfully, I am sure; and I——" he began to feel in his pockets; "I have here a copy of some verses I have written which are to be printed as preface to the volume. I brought them down to Stratford, thinking they would be of interest to thee." He had found the lines by this time in the chaos of his pockets. He pushed back the wine-glasses and cleared his throat portentously, then paused and looked at me anxiously.

"Perchance," he began, "perchance thou dost not

care to hear them. They are faulty lines enough, unworthy of the subject, but, at least, they are written by one who loved Will right dearly."

"And no other apology is needed, if need there be for any," I said, gently. "Proceed, Master Jonson. I know already that the verses will pleasure me greatly."

He cleared his throat again, and began to read in a somewhat pompous tone, although with real feeling. I sat listening, my head resting on my hand. Mingled with Master Jonson's voice were the old, familiar ones of the wind and of the river; the soft sighing of the breeze; the low murmur of the Avon, which always whisper to me one name,—Will, Will, Will.

> "To draw no envy, Shakespeare, on thy name,
> Am I thus ample to thy Book and Fame:
> While I confess thy writings to be such
> As neither Man nor Muse can praise too much."

Thus the stately beginning, followed by lines equaling them in felicity and beauty. How perfect the tribute that came an instant later:

> "Soul of the Age! The applause! delight! the wonder
>   of our Stage!
> My Shakespeare, rise; I will not lodge thee by

Chaucer, or Spenser, or bid Beaumont lie
A little further, to make thee a room:
Thou art a Monument, without a tomb,
And art alive still, while thy Book doth live."

The verses continued, a perfect and gracious tribute from one poet to another. All know them well, yet I will put down the magnificent closing lines, because I love them:

"Sweet Swan of Avon! what a sight it were
To see thee in our waters yet appear,
And make those flights upon the banks of Thames,
That so did take Eliza and our James!
But stay, I see thee in the Hemisphere
Advanc'd, and made a Constellation there!
Shine forth, thou Star of Poets, and with rage,
Or influence, chide, or cheer the drooping Stage;
Which, since thy flight from hence, hath mourn'd like night,
And despaires day, but for thy volumes light."

Master Jonson looked at me as he finished without a trace of his usual noise and bluster.

"Art pleased with the verses, Mistress Shake-speare?" he asked, simply.

22

"They are worthy of Will's dear friend," I answered. "I thank thee, Master Jonson. They are noble lines."

"Then," he said, "since thou art pleased with them, and with the idea of the volume they are to prefix, I am emboldened to tell thee my chief errand to Stratford."

I will not write here what he said next. At first I was so aghast at his proposal that I refused, in a panic at the idea. But, at last, after he had talked long to me, and made me understand his reason for the request, I wavered, then pondered, and finally gave my consent. When he left me, I had begun to look forward to the task.

"His London comrades can speak of him as player and as poet," said Master Jonson. "Thou alone, Mistress Shakespeare, knew him as lover and as man. One other, indeed——" He paused abruptly, and hastily changed his sentence. "This being so, I prythee tell his love story for the world that loves him."

I knew well what his unfinished sentence meant, and who that "one" was to whom he referred. He did not know that I knew, but he will when he reads all I shall write. That Dark Lady of whom he spoke

23

caused me much anguish once; but now, when my life has reached its evening, I can remember even her with pity and forgiveness.

So, obeying Master Jonson, I set about my unaccustomed task. I am not a learned woman; yet I feel no fear, rather a strange confidence. Is it that the theme inspires me; or does Will's spirit enfold and strengthen me as I begin this labor of love? Truly, I do not know; but verily my happiness as I do so is strangely deep and sweet. Here follows, then, my love story and his. 'Tis for the world, and the world may one day forget him, although I think not so. Nay, meseems that the glory he brought to Stratford and to England is not like to fade away; but that Stratford and England will honor forevermore Will Shakespeare, poet and player. Mayhap, however, this is but a fond woman's fancy.

It Was a Lover and His Lass

May Day dawned fair and smiling on Stratford that year; and lads and lasses, as was their wont, rose early to greet it fittingly. As I went about my usual household tasks throughout the morn, I caught glimpses now and again of blithe youths and maidens, decked with flowers, on their way to the Maypole. I heard snatches of gay song and peals of merry laughter, but always from afar. No lad came hastening to Shottery to beg Anne Hathaway as a partner for the Maying. No maiden comrade came to lure her forth to share the merrymaking.

I can scarce say I was grieved that this was so. Such a state of affairs had come to be so much a matter of custom to me that, as a rule, I thought not of it at all. But that May morning something in the spring softness of the air, the sweet freshness of the earth, filled me with that sense of pulsating youth and love which comes even to the sad and solitary at this season.

Conscious of a strange unrest, I found myself, as the
day wore on, by the window. There I stood, gazing
across the fields, with their wealth of spring beauty,
toward the place where Stratford lay fair and smiling
beyond.

There was a strange wistfulness in my heart as I
leaned upon the sill, almost hidden by the clustering
vines. Standing there, I realized, as often before, with
a quiet, sorrowful wonder, how little of the beauty and
the sweetness of life had come to me. Twenty-five May
Days had I seen as child and woman, and from the first
to the present one I had spent them all alike, in solitude
and joylessness. No other lass in Stratford and Shottery, perhaps no other in England, I dared swear could
say the same.

But I knew why; ah, I knew why! I shivered as if
a sudden chill had come to me from the balmy May air,
and I passed my hand drearily across my eyes. In the
room below I heard my grandam stirring about with
a cheerful clatter. She and I alone lived in the cottage
now; but it had not been always so. Six months ago
had ceased to beat the poor restless heart of one who,
while she lived, had made our home, tranquil now, an
evil den of torture. Mad was she, that poor mother of

28

mine, and had been since my earliest remembrance.
Never had I seen, either, my grandam's hair aught but
silvered, although when I was a little child she scarce
could have been a very old woman. I knew now what
had blanched those locks and made her aged before
her time; I realized why I had been transformed into
a grave woman while yet a girl in years. It was the
care of my poor mad mother, sometimes gentle and
harmless, but again brooding, violent, seeking with
devilish cunning to murder us while we slept. Alack!
I knew the very book of madness in its extremest tor-
tures. I conned it, where other children learn happy
and blessed things, at my mother's knee.

What made her mad I never knew until she had
become sane forever. On the night before her burial
I suddenly and softly asked my grandam the question.

"Grandam," I said, "why was it? What drove her
wits astray?"

I was looking down at the dead face, and it was
as if I beheld my own in a glass. The clustering golden
hair was mine, the oval outline of cheek and chin, the
clear pallor of the complexion. The eyes were closed
forever, but in life they had been as dark and sombre
as mine own.

My grandam saw, I think, the resemblance that I noted, and a shudder ran through her, whether at the thought or at my question I knew not. She looked at me with eyes at once fierce and pitiful.

"What makes thee ask that?" she whispered, sharply, and I noticed that her worn and knotted hands were clenched. "What makes thee ask that?"

Sooth, I myself knew not what sudden impulse had prompted the inquiry. I made no answer, but stood as before, gazing into the still dead face, full of that strange, tranquil beauty which death always brings.

Suddenly I was aware that my grandam was gazing at that calm countenance, too, but not quietly, as I was doing. Another moment and a great sob broke the stillness. My grandam fell on her knees beside my mother's body, and tenderly, tremulously, lifted the stark left hand in hers. Then I saw that her shaking finger strove to point out to me something on the still dead hand she held. What was it? For an instant I gazed, uncomprehending. Then suddenly I understood. I looked my sobbing grandam in the eyes searchingly, gravely.

The knowledge that she strove to convey came to

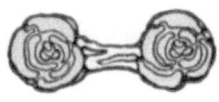

me with a strange sense of familiarity. The dead hand
had no wedding-ring upon it, nor had I recollection of
a father. I was a nameless child.

And that was why, upon this May Day, when the
spring-time called youth and love to make merry, that
I stood alone and sorrowful, while the joy of the world
passed by me, as in a vision far away.

Suddenly another sound broke melodiously across
the low crooning of my grandam in the room below,
across the twitter of the birds without; a sound which
somehow seemed akin to the May Day itself in daunt-
less youth and frank delight. It was a young man's
voice that I heard, mellow and joyous:

> "Her beauty hangs upon the cheek of night
> Like a rich jewel in an Ethiop's ear;
> Beauty too rich for use, for earth too dear."

At the same instant the speaker came in sight. He
looked up and saw me in the window, framed about
with blossoming vines. I knew him at once. It was
young Will Shakespeare.

For a breathless instant we gazed at each other.
I had often passed him in Stratford streets. He knew
my name and my story. We had probably seen each

31

other before a hundred times; but never thus, face to face, on a May morning that made all the world young; never amid sights and sounds that spoke of love alone. In that moment, somehow, some way, all was told. With a strange rush of joy I caught my breath half-sobbingly. I knew that I was no longer solitary and unloved.

As for him, he bared his head and bent it low, just breathing words which I afterwards found were those of his Italian Romeus when he looked on the love of his life:

"It is my lady! Oh, it is my love!"

Then, cap still in hand, he raised his face towards mine, and spoke in more ordinary fashion.

"Mistress Anne, greeting. Wilt come a-Maying with me?"

I was flushed and trembling, and I could not answer at once. I realized that he had used the commonplace words to still my agitation; but I could not immediately avail myself of his consideration.

"Nay," I faltered at length; "I—I——" There I paused, and my face grew suddenly crimson. I remembered who and what I was. What right had I to such

32

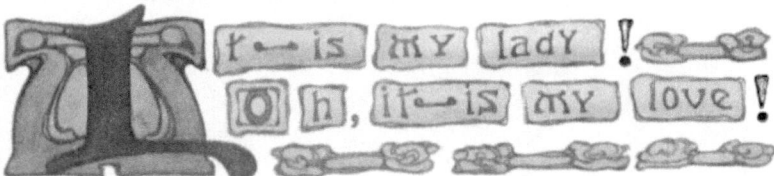

It is my lady! Oh, it is my love!

joy? Moreover, he was a mere, happy lad; I a sad, mature woman. The hard thought thrust itself upon me unbidden. There were numberless fair Stratford maidens, among whom he could find a more fitting May Day sweetheart.

"Thou dost forget," I said at length, still faltering, although I strove to speak coldly; "thou dost forget. It is——" I hesitated, then went on hurriedly; "it is necessity that isolates me. It is thy choice that thou art solitary."

He must have known my meaning at once, for my story was familiar in Stratford; but he replied instantly.

"Sweet Mistress Anne," he said, and his voice was, if possible, a shade more courteous than before, "believe me, thou art the only lass that I desire to go a-Maying with me. If thou dost refuse me I will go solitary still."

There was that in his manner which suggested more than his words; which told me that he wished my company for a much longer period than a spring day, and that if I did not yield, his loneliness would be for all his life. I hesitated, my mind in a whirl. Impetuously, he leaped the gate, clambered up the

trellis work over which the vines grew and brought his face at last on a level with mine own.

"Anne," he breathed in tones so silver sweet as to melt the hardest woman's heart; "dear Mistress Anne, surely thou dost know, surely dost understand, that I—ah, what need of words? And yet—oh, Anne, dearest, stand not silent there, with the color flaming into thy dear fair face. I am envious of the very vines that screen thee. Say but three words, sweet, and make Will Shakespeare happy forevermore!"

In the midst of his impetuous pleading there came to me the recollection of my thoughts a half hour since; the memory of the mad presence that had haunted my childhood and girlhood; the vision of my poor mother's ringless hand——

I turned from the window. He reached forward and laid his hand on mine as it rested upon the sill. The touch was light, but insistent, imperative.

"Thou dost forget——" I whispered again, falteringly, looking at him with pleading eyes, "thou dost forget. There is—there is a shadow on my life. Oh, haste thee from me, lest it fall likewise on thee."

His lips rested on my hand for an instant.

"Ay, sweetheart," he said, and I could never tell

half the tenderness that spoke in his voice; "ay, I do forget it, as thou, too, shalt forget. I will give thee a key to release thee from thy prison of gloom and sorrow; a key of three parts. 'Tis 'I love thee,' Nan. Say it, sweetheart, sweetheart. Say only now, 'I love thee'; then come with me from out the shadows into sunlight forevermore."

Chapter III

he **Course** of **True Love**

And so, good sooth, was lifted the heavy pall that had lain over my youth and happiness, and what was seeming dead arose to glorious resurrection. "Forevermore!" Will had said. "Come with me from out the shadows into sunlight forevermore!" Ah, thou didst speak truly, thou dear light of my life! Though clouds have often sought to darken the eternal brightness of thy love, behind them still its radiance hath never ceased to shine; will shine forever.

For a month after that most joyous May Day none knew of our love. In this matter Will bowed to my wish. Many saw us together during the afternoon, and marveled thereat; but the excitements of the day were many, and our companionship was speedily forgot. When, our Maying ended, Will brought me home, he said, as we parted at the gate:

"To-morrow, sweetheart, to-morrow wilt thou come with me to my parents as my promised bride?

Our formal betrothal shall follow as speedily as may be; our marriage when thou wilt."

I was silent for a moment. The soft, star-lit night seemed to whisper calm and confidence, yet my heart was far from quiet.

"Nay," I said, suddenly, wistfully, "thou dost not know me, although our faces have been familiar to each other these many years. For a month—a month—let me keep my happy secret. Then, if thou dost desire still to—to wed me——"

He flung himself upon his knee before me, and, in knightly fashion, kissed my hand. "As thou wilt," he said. "But if me no ifs, thou cruel fair. One month, then, from to-night—see, sweet Nan, the round moon rises yonder, and by yonder blessed moon I swear——" I laid my finger upon his lips.

"The moon changes," I said, half laughing, half in earnest; "she changes monthly, Will. Swear not by the moon, lest, like her, thy love prove variable."

"Then name the oath," he begged, still kneeling.

"Nay," said I; "no oath is needed. Swear not at all; or, if thou wilt——" my voice grew suddenly passionate—"swear by thyself, thy dear and gracious self. Ah, Will, God forgive thee if thou dost play me false!"

He sprang up instantly in indignant denial, pouring forth vows and fond words. I listened and believed him, as is weak woman's wont. The evening fled on wings. The round moon rose higher and higher in the heavens. When he left me, at length, his betrothal kiss was upon my lips, his promise given to keep our love secret for a month, as I desired.

Ah, what a month it was that followed!

What wanderings had we through the Stratford fields! What new music we found in the song of the birds, what fresh sweetness in the flowers! The voices of the wind and the river, ever eloquent to him, spoke also through him to me. Ofttimes the Avon and I have listened to the stories that the world knows now. The dear stream seemed to sigh with Juliet or laugh with Rosalind. Methought it hushed its babble as the spirit of Prince Hamlet passed, wrapped in ineffable mystery; and sobbed in stormy trouble as poor mad Lear rushed by.

We learned to know each other, too. Will heard of my sad childhood, my shadowed girlhood, and swore in tender wrath that never should I know sorrow more. I learned of his far different past; a childhood of plenty; a youth, which, although not altogether care-free, was

yet blessed with a happy home. His father was one
of Stratford's most honored citizens; his mother, a
stately dame of ancient family. I have said that his
youth was not altogether care-free; nor was it; for he
was tormented by increasing poverty as he grew older.
His father's affairs became, at length, hopelessly en-
tangled, and Will was obliged to seek some means of
livelihood. Not having been educated with any expec-
tation of such a necessity, he found it hard to choose
an occupation. He had tried his hand at many things
before I met him. For a while he was lawyer's clerk.
Later he left the desk to become apprentice to a butcher,
who offered higher wages. Yet again he occupied the
schoolmaster's chair. When we met, however, he had
at length decided on the life-work that was destined to
bring him both fame and wealth, although as yet he
had had no opportunity of adopting it. Other Stratford lads had gone to London, and had won success as
players. A poet and a player he would be, then, and
strive thus to restore his family's fortunes.

All his dreams, all his plans, he confided to me, as
we wandered through the fields or sat in my grandam's
little garden. The great of history and legend bore us
company, too, and whispered of a time to come when

42

they would live for all the world. Meanwhile the mystery of Will's love was mine, and we were happy in each other.

At last the month ended. Strangely, safely, our secret had been kept. None knew, or so we thought, why Will came so frequently to Shottery. None dreamed that he had any attraction there save the spring beauty of the fields and woods he was known to love well. Come what might, that month was ours forever.

The round moon was rising again as it had risen that night of our Maying. I stood at the gate as I had stood then, watching for Will's arrival. As I waited there my grandam came out and joined me.

Now, during the month just completed I had frequently noticed that my grandam never let me far from her sight. She must have conjectured, of course, the state of affairs between Will and me, although I had not actually told her of our happiness. So unobtrusive had been her constant presence that Will had marked it not at all. When I saw her lingering about us I thought that her life, which had held so little joy and peace, was brightened by the sight of our love and happiness. The sequel proved me wrong.

43

I was surprised when she joined me at the gate; for, though never far apart in the cottage, we seldom sought each other's company. I was still more surprised when she spoke first, for she was a woman of few words.

"It is a clear and beauteous night," she observed, calmly, glancing up at the moon; "but the summer is still young, and it is damp here at the gate. Dost wait for young Shakespeare, Nan?"

She asked the question in the same tone in which she had commented upon the beauty of the night. I flushed a little at her matter-of-fact manner.

"Ay, grandam," I said, dutifully.

"He hath never yet failed thee," she went on, looking at me strangely; "and yet he is late to-night, Anne, very late."

"He will come," I said, proudly, and turned away from her.

She paused a moment, and the searching gaze she fixed upon me brought back my eyes unwillingly to her face.

"Hath he——" she hesitated a little, and now her voice was full of suppressed feeling; "hath he ever said aught to thee of—marriage?"

44

I looked her proudly in the eyes, and I felt my face aflame. "Ay," I said, hotly; "ay, from the first. A month ago he would have betrothed me, but I besought him to wait."

My grandam's bosom rose and fell with a quick breath of relief, but when she spoke her voice was cold again.

"Thou fool!" she said, calmly. "Thou didst beseech him to wait! Thou fool!"

She paused an instant. I opened my lips to reply, but my indignation choked me. Before I found words she continued:

"Thou art a fool, but why do I blame thee? Thou scarce canst help it. Thy mother was the like. I did not know her folly until too late." Her voice broke a little, but hardened again as she resumed, "I do know thine—I trust to heaven in time. I hope wisdom will not reach thee when it will avail thee not." And with that she turned and went into the cottage.

As the door closed upon her I felt two hands clasped across my eyes.

"Thou must guess," said a voice I knew well, rich with laughter. "The penalty's a kiss if thou dost not know. Guess who blinds thee!"

45

I named his name in tones that quivered a little. He heard my tremulous answer, he felt the tears in my eyes, and his voice changed instantly.

"What ails thee, sweeting? Why dost weep? Share thy sorrow with me."

But this I could not do, although he begged me sorely. My grandam's words had been harsh, but they were kindly meant and she had deemed them deserved. I could not repeat them to Will, for they would show lack of trust in him. Besides, my sorrow was ended now he had come. I told him so, smiling my tears away.

He shook his head when I evaded an answer to his entreating, but yielded to my desire. "I have a story to tell thee," he said, gravely. "Before I begin let me ask thee to believe that I would not beg of thee the boon that I shall crave, seemed it not best for thee. Thou knowest Sir Thomas Lucy?"

I looked at him askance at this abrupt changing of the subject, and I nodded.

"Everyone knows Sir Thomas," I said. "Had he been given his way the Maypole would have been cut down and the players would not be coming to Stratford next week. He is a Puritan of the Puritans, Will. Why dost thou speak of him now?"

"For many reasons, sweetheart," Will answered; "but chiefly because—the tale is long. Wilt go within?"

"Nay," I said, hurriedly, bitterly. "Nay, I will not within; speak on."

He glanced at me as if puzzled by my tone, but said nothing about it then. In a rapid, low voice he told his story, interrupting himself now and again to laugh at some reminiscence of the past or at some plan for the future.

Sir Thomas Lucy, the pompous, Puritanical owner of Charlcote, had strictly forbidden the stealing of deer from his Park. This I knew, and also that the law, although just, was scarce generous; for it had been a tradition in his family to allow a certain number of deer each twelve-month for the use of the people of the surrounding country. This unwritten compact with the commoners Sir Thomas had set aside, thereby arousing wonder, and later wrath, among them. At first the countryfolk had been unable to believe Sir Thomas in earnest, and deer continued to disappear now and then from the Park. Finally, however, the wrath of the knight had blazed high at the continued disregard of his decree. One or two Stratford lads had been arrested several days before on the charge of deer-

stealing. Therefore, to-morrow night all loyal Stratford youths——

At this point, in the interest of his narrative, Will's voice unconsciously rose. So absorbed was I in what he was saying that I scarce noted the fact, but afterwards I realized that it had been so. Had I looked back then, I imagine, I should have seen my grandam somewhere near. But I did not look, and Will thought not of any auditor save myself.

"Therefore, Nan," he said, "the brave lads of Stratford have planned a vengeance to rebuke the churlish knight. To-morrow evening we meet at Charlcote and go a-hunting, sweetheart, but not for deer alone. And when we have found our game we will sing for Sir Thomas that little song of mine:

"What shall he have that killed the deer?"

He carolled the line lustily, then broke into a laugh.

"Sir Thomas will long remember that hunting, methinks."

He paused a moment, then looked at me anxiously.

"The moon hath gone behind a cloud, sweet Nan, and the light is dim; yet soothly, I can read disapproval in thy face. 'Tis a rough joke enough; but truly the

knight deserves that it be played upon him. Natheless, I should not have told thee of it, not troubled thee with the story, except——"

He paused again, then came closer to me and put his arm about me.

"Sweetheart," he said, "beyond Charlcote there is a priest, and we can find two witnesses among the Stratford lads. To-day the month ends, dear Nan. To-morrow, wilt be mine forever?"

I clung to him in silence, and for an instant could not speak. He went on rapidly, gently.

"Sooth, I were proud to wed thee, dear, before all the world; but who knows, who knows what may befall? Besides—daily my family's affairs grow more straitened. If the players come next week, I may perchance go with them back to London. Such an opportunity might not occur again. Before I go I would have thee safely mine, dear heart; and a wedding after the usual fashion would take long to arrange."

He paused again. Still I could not speak.

"Nan, Nan," he went on, passionately, "God wot, I grieve sore to ask this of thee, yet I see no other way. For this once trust me, sweetheart, and listen to my plan. The sport will be rough and fast to-morrow

49

night at Charlcote. While it is at its height we can slip away, find the priest, and——"

"But," I faltered forth at length, "but how can I go with thee?"

"I will bring horses hither," Will answered without an instant's hesitation. He had evidently thought out the plan most carefully. "A long cloak shall disguise thee effectually enough, for thou wilt not be long among the rest. Then, after we are wedded, I will bring thee home at once."

"My grandam——" I whispered.

Will looked at me in surprise.

"Thy grandam?" he repeated. "Thou wilt tell her, of course. She surely hath guessed what lies between us. Tell her, by all means. To-morrow night at this hour will I come for thee, bringing the cloak and the horses. What say'st, Nan? Wilt be ready, sweet?"

I felt his firm, tender hand on mine. Ah, how could I hesitate an instant? I raised my face to his and spoke, forgetting all else: "I shall be ready; and whither thou wilt, I shall go, my beloved."

I heard him give a quick breath of relief.

"It is well," he said, and kissed me. "I will not fail thee, sweetheart; and may God speed our plan!"

Chapter. IV

# Under the Greenwood Tree

All was still in the house, and the door of my grandam's room was closed, when, an hour later, I went to bed. I hesitated beside her chamber a moment, half-minded to go in and tell her of our plan; but it was late; all was quiet. I went on to my own room, resolving to reveal all in the morning.

I had uneasy dreams that night, and once I awakened with a start, quite certain that I had heard the cautious opening and closing of a door. I listened attentively for several moments, but heard nothing; and I concluded that I must have been dreaming. When at length I fell asleep again my slumber was sound, and I did not awaken until much later than was my wont. Dismayed that the sun had moved so high, I dressed hurriedly and ran down-stairs. My grandam was nowhere to be seen.

For a while I stood dismayed at her absence, all sorts of wild conjectures floating through my brain. But presently I calmed myself. My grandam often

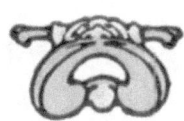

went into Stratford to the innkeeper, Mistress Quickly, to sell the produce of our garden. This was probably what she had done this morning. Sometimes she spent the night at the inn. If she did so this time, nothing of our marriage need be said to her until I chose. If she returned early or late in the evening, however, and found me gone—I dismissed the fear with an effort. All was pointing towards a happy consummation of our plans. I would not imagine trouble. Speed onward, happy day, and bring the joyous night!

The hours went by and my grandam came not. Evening arrived and still there were no signs of her. At length, with trembling fingers, I dressed myself in my darkest gown and sat down to await Will's coming.

I had not long to wait. Promptly at moonrise I heard the clatter of hoofs, next his familiar quick footstep on the path below. I went to meet him.

"Art ready?" he whispered. "That's brave. Come. Here is thy cloak." He wrapped it about me with rapid, skillful fingers, then put on a similar one himself. So closely were we muffled that one could not tell which was man, which maid. Even after we had mounted, Will paused and arranged the draperies so that the distinction would still be hard to make.

Once on horseback, I forgot my tremors. The night was very lovely. There was a June softness in the air. The round moon smiled upon us. The friendly stars brightened our pathway. The scent of roses made the evening faintly sweet, mysterious. And through this brightness and sweetness I rode with my true lover at my side, and forgot all else.

Arriving at the Charlcote gates, at last, we dismounted cautiously, and Will led the horses to some distance before tying them. Then he returned to me, and spoke low and rapidly:

"Keep thy cloak well about thee, and come, dear Nan. I must show myself to the lads, that they may see I am faithful to the compact. They are not aware of thy presence, nor need they know who thou art. Follow, and trust to me."

A moment later we arrived in the midst of a silent, cautiously-moving group which had evidently been awaiting Will's arrival. He quickly gave a few suggestions and commands, obeying which the crowd scattered in various directions. At the house all were to meet, bring Sir Thomas Lucy forth and clap upon his head the horns from one of the stolen deer, while the lads sang Will's derisive verses. The plan had been

arranged before. It took but a few moments to start the youths on their way to the house. Will waited until the last; then turned to me.

"Now, Nan, now is our time. They will deem that I have deserted them, but all can be explained later. I have asked two of my comrades to join us at a certain point; I did not say for what reason, but I know they will keep tryst. Come, then, sweetheart, let us hasten to the meeting-place. The Charlcote woods await us in the moonlight; such woods as these surely are not in all England else, Nan. See how the sweet night doth gently kiss the trees, and look how the floor of heaven is thick inlaid with patines of bright gold."

So talking, he hurried me along, peopling the forest for me, as often before, with the creatures of his fancy.

"Canst not almost see the fairies, Nan?" he said. "That mossy bank is fit to be the couch of Queen Titania herself. Mark those lights that thou seest flicker hither and yon. They are not glow-worms, Nan, as thou might'st think; but King Oberon and his elves, who are flitting there. See yon bat! his flight's impeded by a fairy on his back. Would we had more time to search beneath these nodding blossoms; for there the sprites sleep, airily and soft. And yonder——"

A sudden loud confusion of voices broke across his murmured fancies and put an end to the peace of the perfect night. Will stopped short.

"What has happened?" he cried, half to himself, half to me. "Surely, the plan could not fail. Nan, stay here until I join thee. We are near the meeting-place that I appointed." And with that he darted off through the woods like an arrow.

But for once I disobeyed him. After him I followed as rapidly as I could, for I was encumbered by my cloak, and went far enough to see him at length rush forward and join in the yelling, confused mêlée that pushed and swore and shouted just outside the door of the mansion. I paused on the edge of the Park, within the shadow of a tree.

I saw in an instant that Sir Thomas had not been captured. The reverse seemed to be the case; for I noted that several of the Stratford lads had their arms bound, while the knight stood pompously on the steps, apparently giving directions as to the disposal of his prisoners. The struggle between those who had not yet been overpowered and the knight's servants still continued, and the issue seemed doubtful. Will rushed at once into the thick of the fight, and I loved him the

better for not deserting his comrades in their peril. His arrival seemed to give the rest new courage, and they struggled desperately to escape capture; but it was a vain endeavor. Many as they were, the knight's men outnumbered them three to one. One by one the Stratford lads were overpowered, lastly even Will. He made a fierce endeavor to conquer his captors, and his strength seemed almost preternatural. I knew why. He thought of me, waiting for him among the trees, and of our plans for the happy ending to this night's frolic. But at last, even he was overcome.

Two burly knaves bore him to the earth with a shout of triumph. For a moment he ceased to struggle, and he lay as if dead. When I saw that I forgot all else. I remembered not who nor where I was. I saw only Will lying stark upon the ground. I sped forward from the tree's friendly shadow, and the next instant found myself, I scarce knew how, kneeling beside him. There was a sudden calm in the tumult about me. All eyes were fixed upon my face in wonder. But to me it was as if Will and I were alone. The rest seemed as shadows. I heard my own voice like some one's else, sobbing and calling his name.

Chapter V

O Cursed Spire

"Ha! what means this?" I heard Sir Thomas Lucy exclaim, as, realizing on the instant the imprudence of my action, I cowered down beside Will, muffling my face in my cloak. "Seize him, varlets, seize him! What new villainy is this?"

Two stout men stepped forward immediately. Ere they reached me, however, attention was diverted from me. As if knowing that I had need of him, Will stirred, opened his eyes in dazed fashion, then sat upright. The next moment, comprehending the situation in a flash, he was on his feet.

"Nay," he cried, standing between me and the glare of the torches, and making a quick gesture betwixt command and appeal; "nay, I protest, Sir Thomas Lucy. This friend is no Stratford lad, and hath not taken part in this night's business. Prythee, therefore, bid thy servants forbear!"

Will's body shielding me, I raised my head breathlessly and peeped at Sir Thomas with wide eyes of apprehension. The torches' light shone full upon him,

and revealed a look of satisfied malice and sneering triumph on his pale, puritanical face.

"Aha!" he said, slowly, replying to Will. "A friend, say'st? A friend of thine, most like; a poor recommendation! What ho! More torches there!"

Will had done his best to shield me and had failed. He gave a deep, despairing sigh as the lights came flashing towards us. I rose, trembling, my cloak still wrapped about me. But again a diversion occurred. The heavy door behind Sir Thomas opened ponderously; and on its threshold appeared three unexpected figures; Lady Lucy, Mistress Mary Shakespeare, and —my grandam.

At sight of them I stood as if turned to stone. I had nerved myself to meet exposure and recognition; but I had not expected treachery. Will made no sign of surprise. He stood immovable, his arms folded. Sir Thomas shot a quick glance at us both; then gave a rapid order to his servants. In reply, the latter began the difficult task of removing the captive Stratford lads to the house for safe-keeping. 'Twas an arduous duty that they strove to perform, for their prisoners were most unruly. The air was filled with mocking protests, profane threatenings, and rough jests at Sir Thomas's

expense. These last made the knight turn purple with
rage, and he was restrained from setting upon the saucy
knaves himself only by the cries and pleadings of his
lady. Finally, however, the task was accomplished.
The last Stratford lad was forced into the house by his
captors, the great door closed upon them all, and a
brief lull ensued.

Sir Thomas, choking and sputtering with anger, at
length managed to regain some slight measure of self-
control. When he had reached this point, he put his
lady impatiently aside and beckoned to Will and me.
At the summons Will offered me his hand in silence.
I laid my cold fingers within his. So, like two children,
we went forward to meet our fate.

"Will Shakespeare," began Sir Thomas, pompously, as we finally came to a standstill before him;
" 'tis a mad and vicious deed that thou didst plan this
night. The Lord be praised that thou wast hindered
from carrying it out."

Will gazed at him without a word. The knight's
whining piety was so obviously an outer crust of his
real nature. 'Twas a convenient coat to show a goodly
outside to the world; but within there dwelt how poor
and mean a soul!

"Thou hast done me good service, Dame Hathaway," the knight continued, condescendingly, turning to my grandam. He was evidently somewhat confused by Will's steadfast, scornful eyes. "I shall not forget it, and——"

"The service is Mistress Shakespeare's as well as mine," responded my grandam, her eyes fixed full upon my face. "I told her of the plot I overheard; and it was by her advice that I came hither to seek thy worship. I trust that thou wilt not forget the promise thou didst make, that my grand-daughter's share in this escapade shall remain unknown except to those here present. This boon, Sir Thomas, thou hast granted me in return for my warning. As for Master Shakespeare, his mother must speak. She learned to-day, for the first, of her son's entanglement with my grand-daughter."

"And heard it to my sorrow and shame," added Mistress Shakespeare, in a low, clear voice, so like Will's that my heart was strangely stirred. "I had deemed my son a man of honor, worthy of his Arden blood. Never before in all his life hath he been guilty of deception, nor concealed aught from me."

Then, indeed, Will started as if stung. He made an impetuous step towards her.

"Sweet mother," he began, eagerly, imploringly, "dear lady, say not so. Thou know'st not all. I could not tell thee sooner. Indeed, indeed, deception and dishonor were far from my thoughts. I have longed for the day when I could bring her to thee, could give thee a daughter——"

His mother made a gesture of abhorrence, and cast a fleeting, scornful glance at me.

"Thou didst intend to marry her!" she said, slowly, and the disdain in her voice cut me to the very heart. "This passes! Thou wouldst have taken as thy wedded wife this madwoman's daughter, this bastard——"

Will's imperative, uplifted hand made her pause; his eyes blazed with anger. He turned from Mistress Shakespeare and drew me to his breast with an exquisite movement of protection.

"By that speech thou hast lost a son, mother," he said, quietly, and the calm decision of his words was more effective than any storm of rage. Then he spoke to me, with infinite tenderness. "Thou hearest, beloved! 'Tis as I feared, and yet I hoped also. This is why I sought to wed thee as I did. All my life shall recompense thee for those words, sweetheart!"

His voice was low, but perfectly distinct. His

mother turned scarlet, and the tears rushed to her eyes. Despising me before, surely she hated me now. But Will's self-control was an inheritance. She turned calmly to Sir Thomas.

"Do with him as thou wilt. Some madness soothly affects him or some potent spell hath bewitched him. Strive, prythee, to bring him to his senses. Dame Hathaway, I thank thee for thy warning. Lady Lucy, I crave thy hospitality for the night. On the morrow I will return to Stratford."

So saying, with a stately curtsey to Sir Thomas and Lady Lucy, and a gracious inclination to my grandam, Mistress Shakespeare entered the house.

The knight cleared his throat pompously as she disappeared.

"A foolish son is the heaviness of his mother," he observed, sanctimoniously, rolling his eyes heavenward; "and the way of the transgressor is hard. Thy sin hath found thee out, Will Shakespeare, and——"

"Waste no words, Sir Thomas," said Will, interrupting him unceremoniously; "I am in thy power, as thou knowest right well. Do with me as thou wilt."

The knight opened his mouth to utter another high-sounding sentence, but this time, to my surprise,

66

my grandam interposed. Her face was white, and her voice sounded curiously husky.

"Sir Thomas," she said, "thou hast said that I have done thee good service this night. I have now a further boon to crave than the one thou hast already granted me. Prythee, let me speak to these two for a brief space in private."

Sir Thomas looked at her, amazed; but her face was inscrutable. He muttered to himself for a moment, gazing upon her with suspicion; but finally his countenance cleared. She had indeed done him a great service. The favor she asked was a harmless one. His triumph over his enemies had been so complete that he could afford to be somewhat magnanimous.

"Have thy wish," he said at length, albeit somewhat ungraciously. "I will remain just within. If he should attempt escape, one call will suffice to bring me." And with that he made his exit, his lady fluttering about him like a bird around its mate.

The instant he was gone, Will's self-restraint flew to the winds. He caught me yet closer to him, murmuring passionate caressing words, explanations, apologies. It was as if he could not do enough to make amends for his mother's cruel scorn.

67

"But stay," he said, suddenly checking himself; "the time is brief. Tell me, sweetheart, tell me that thou dost trust me still. Oh, never fear, dear love; happiness shall yet be ours, and this past woe shall seem to us as naught. See, Nan," and he gently turned my face towards the tranquil scene beyond; "see where Charlcote lies in the moonlight, calm and heavenly fair. Even so, one day, shall be our wedded bliss, Nan, dear Nan, my sweetheart, my wife!"

I murmured a tender word or two, and laid my hands in his with perfect trust. Past troubles, future perplexities, were as naught. He bent his head and kissed me.

"Light of my life, I thank thee. A time will come, I hope, when thy trust shall be rewarded; a time when thou wilt be proud that thou art Shakespeare's sweetheart."

"Of that she is proud now," said a low voice behind us. We turned with a start. We had entirely forgotten my grandam's presence. "She is proud now, and well she may be," she added, to my complete surprise. Will looked at her sternly.

"Why thou didst choose to play the spy I know not, Dame Hathaway," he said, somewhat bitterly.

"Methinks thou didst do so scarce effectually. I brought thy grand-daughter here this night, meaning to take her back to Shottery as my wedded wife. That she is not such at this moment is thine own fault, and thine alone."

"Ay," answered my grandam, in an odd, breathless tone, and her hands made a strange wavering movement as if she besought his pardon; "ay, so I heard thee tell thy mother. I have wronged thee, Will Shakespeare, wronged thee much. I crave thy forgiveness. I had a daughter once—'tis an old story. Well, I feared lest that daughter's daughter——" She paused abruptly.

"I cannot make amends," she went on presently; "yet I can at least explain, and hope for the future. 'Tis true, I overheard but part of thy plans. I understood that Nan was coming hither with thee, and that she would be the only woman present. Ere thou hadst gone I slipped away to Stratford and told thy mother all I knew. She was amazed and displeased, as thou hast seen, and advised that Sir Thomas Lucy be warned. When I returned to Shottery it was very late. Thou hadst gone and Nan had retired to her chamber. I had left my door closed, that she might think I slept within. When I returned from my interview with thy mother,

I opened it most cautiously, yet it creaked villainously, and again when I closed it. Didst hear it, Nan?"

"Ay," I answered; "but thought it a dream. I had no idea that thou wert not in the house when I sought my room."

"To-day," my grandam went on, "I went to Mistress Shakespeare as we had planned, and we came together to Sir Thomas with our story. I meant all for the best; wilt not believe it, Nan? Wilt not believe it, Master Shakespeare? Sir Thomas has promised me that Nan's share in this night's doings shall remain a secret. When thy punishment is over——"

"Ay, when," Will said, more gloomily than I had ever heard him speak. "Sir Thomas is not a man to forgive easily, nor to punish lightly."

"But he cannot do more than imprison thee," my grandam urged. "And when thou art free——"

What sudden impulse caused the thought I know not, but at that moment an idea occurred to me.

"Free!" I whispered. "Never fear, Will, thou shalt be free soon. I know a way."

He shook his head. "What thou mean'st I know not, sweetheart; but free I shall be one day, assuredly, and until then——"

The great door creaked and we heard Sir Thomas Lucy's voice. Will turned hurriedly to my grandam and spoke with sudden passion:

"Dame Hathaway, I trust thee; I must perforce. Guard her for me until I may make her mine; and God forgive thee if thou dost play us false!"

 oor — Players

The next morning at dawn my grandam and I returned to Shottery. We traversed the way on foot, and for the most part in silence. What had become of the two horses that Will had left on the borders of the Park was a mystery to me then. Afterwards I learned that one of Sir Thomas's servants had captured them as spoils of war. That we walked in silence was no surprise to me, for my grandam was, as I have said, a woman of few words. Her flow of conversation to Will and me on the terrace had astonished me. Only sudden and great reason could have so stirred her to speech.

The night before, I had galloped on horseback along this same road in its moonlit beauty. To-day in the dreary dawn I dragged my laggard feet towards home. Yet all was not dark. My grandam and Will had reached an understanding; and my idea, the sudden, hopeful thought that had come to me the night before, still stayed with me and animated my weary spirits.

My grandam said naught of this, nor of anything

75

else. She had relapsed again into her ordinary mood of calm self-possession. Only once did she speak to me. That was when we stood again at the door of our cottage.

"The way was long and weary," she said, looking at me with a new softness in her eyes; "but take courage, Nan. The sun hath risen."

I understood the double meaning she intended to convey.

"Ay, grandam," I answered, gently; "but for me the sun rose forever a month since, when Will Shakespeare first told me of his love."

And with that we entered the cottage, and, without speaking further, began our morning tasks.

The day passed slowly, but evening came at last, and with it a neighbor who brought us tidings of Will and his friends. The knight's wrath had blazed high at his repeated injuries, and all the lads were sentenced to varying terms of imprisonment. Will, being the ringleader, was doomed to the longest captivity.

The news was not unexpected, so neither my grandam nor I evinced great surprise. When, disappointed at our lack of emotion, the gossip had gone to spread the news elsewhere, I said:

76

"Have the players come yet to Stratford, grandam?"

"Nay, lass, but they arrive to-morrow," she answered. "When I was in the town yesterday Dame Quickly was making great preparations. They are huge feeders, she says."

"I wonder," I said, reflectively, "I wonder if she would care to have me go to help her. I have done so before when she was hard pressed."

"Ay, I think likely, since thou art a favorite of hers," my grandam answered. "Why dost wish to go?"

But I did not desire yet to tell my real reason, even to her.

"The extra coins she pays me will not come amiss," I answered, evasively; "and I should like to see the players. I have never yet beheld them."

"Then go when thou wilt, lass," said my grandam. "To-morrow morn, if thou desirest. Dame Quickly will welcome thee, I know."

Before we slept that night it was agreed that I should do this, and I went to bed well pleased.

The town was all astir when I entered it next day. The coming of the players always formed one of the few great excitements in Stratford. The inn, especially, I found in bustle and excitement, and as my

grandam had predicted, Dame Quickly welcomed me with effusion. The players were expected in the afternoon, and I was set to making a huge pasty for their delectation.

How many hopes and fears, what tremors and confidences, went into that pasty along with the materials that composed it! So far my sudden plan had prospered well. Would I be able to carry it yet further?

I put my best skill into the making of the pasty, and it looked most inviting when I had finished. Dame Quickly was so delighted with its success that I was emboldened to take my second step in the pathway I had planned for myself.

"Wilt let me wait on the table, Mistress Quickly? I would like well to see the players."

She pursed up her lips and looked at me critically, kindly.

"Thou art—well, if thou wilt have it, thou art too comely, Nan," she said at length. "They are loose, rough men, some of them. Thy golden hair, thy large eyes, thy smooth skin would captivate their eyes—perhaps to thine own hurt. I should never forgive myself shouldst thou meet harm through me."

78

I flushed rosily, both at the suggestion of her words and at the admiration they conveyed. What woman loves not to hear that she is beautiful?

"I will strive to conduct myself properly," I said, demurely, "and if they prove too boisterous I can come to thee. Prythee let me do it, dame. I have heard so much of the players and have never seen them."

Somewhat reluctantly she promised, and my heart leaped with delight. Another part of my self-imposed task was accomplished.

A few hours later, loud shouting and the blare of trumpets heralded the arrival of the players. The whole town turned out to welcome them, and amid a storm of huzzas, greetings and jests they rode into Stratford, and alighted at the door of the inn.

When they had actually arrived, I was seized for an instant with a perfect agony of apprehension. There seemed to be so many of them; they were so big and boisterous. How could I ever carry out my plan?

Dame Quickly's voice calling me brought me back to my senses. I thought of Will and grew strong. I went to obey the summons, and found that my duties were to begin at once, since the players had arrived ravenous. Dame Quickly had put them into a room

by themselves, with one huge table for them all, and she bade me hasten, since they were impatient for their wine.

As I stood on the threshold of the room an instant, gathering up my courage for an entrance, I heard a melodious voice within carolling out a catch which the others were interrupting without the least ceremony:

"Which is the happiest day to drink?"

sang forth the mellow tones.

"How can I name one day?"

roared the chorus.

"Tuesday, Wednesday, Thursday, Friday,
Saturday, Sunday, Monday!"

shouted the whole noisy company.

I pushed open the door and entered. To my astonishment and confusion, at my appearance instant silence fell. I almost dropped the cups I held, in my embarrassment.

"Hebe, and no other," cried the same rich, careless

voice that had been singing. "By St. George, where gat the little town this daughter of the gods?"

"Hist, Marlowe," interposed a gentler voice. "The maid is modest, and thou dost trouble her."

"Modest, and a tavern wench!" cried a coarser player, who sat near the door. "Impossible! Come and kiss me, pretty sweeting!"

"Nay," called the one who had spoken in my favor; "nay, let be, Kyd. Prythee bring the cups hither, mistress, an it please thee."

The tone was deferential, yet gently admonitory.

I ventured to raise my eyes, as I obeyed. The speaker I recognized instantly, although he was some years older than when I had seen him, a lad in Stratford streets. 'Twas Dick Burbadge, who had been my champion. He beckoned to me to bring the cups, and as I obediently set them before him, he murmured so that none could hear: "I know not who thou art; but this is no place for a modest maid, and such thou seemest. Ask Dame Quickly to send another in thy place."

Now was my chance, or never. I answered, breathlessly and low, "I have a reason for being here. Let me speak with thee privately."

81

He glanced at me, surprised, but my strong desire must have shown in my face, for he nodded almost on the instant.

"Be it so. I will watch for an opportunity. Go hence now."

"Take that, Kit Marlowe!" suddenly cried a shrill, angry voice that I had not heard as yet; and the speaker, a slender, petulant-looking youth, followed his speech by a box on Marlowe's ear. "Why wilt thou treat me like a fool? I am no woman, in sooth, though I may act a woman's part."

"How now! What is the dispute?" asked Burbadge, who seemed to be peacemaker in general for the company.

"Nay," drawled Marlowe in his rich, lazy voice, "I did but beg my lady here to press her lips upon the cup ere I drank from it. As Ben Jonson hath it:

> "Drink to me only with thine eyes,
> And I will pledge with mine;
> Or leave a kiss within the cup,
> And I'll not look for wine.

"I'm practising for the play, Dick, that is all."
The youth he was teasing gave an angry flounce.

"Robin, Robin Greene, dost not know Kit by this time?" said Burbadge, his grave face relaxing into a smile.

"I care not," replied Greene, still petulantly. "He shall not flout me, as if I were no man. I am slender, indeed, and my beard is scant; yet I can drink any one of you under the table, I'll wager my purse."

"Ay, I warrant," said Burbadge, with something like a sigh. "Were Jonson here, he'd have a classical allusion to illustrate that same wager of thine."

"Which is the happiest day to drink?"

carolled Marlowe again, winking at Greene insolently; and under cover of the vociferous chorus that followed I made my exit.

I went and told Dame Quickly that I found the company e'en too boisterous for my taste, whereat she nodded her head wisely and sent her homeliest maid in my place. I followed her as far as the door and stood there quaking, wondering if Burbadge could and would keep his promise. The instant red-cheeked Sukey entered the room I heard an uproar of voices, then a crash of breaking glass, followed by her unceremonious exit in tears. The next instant Burbadge

came out, also. As he did so the noise within subsided.

"They will have none but thee," he said, hurriedly, breathlessly. "They refused to let the other wench wait upon them. They threw the china on the floor in anger. Thou must e'en come, I fear; but I will see that thou dost not meet with insult. First, however, what dost thou want with me? I said I would find and bring thee. I did so that I might have the opportunity of speaking with thee privately, as thou didst desire."

"Oh, sir," I began, hurriedly, clasping my hands in passionate entreaty, " 'tis about Will Shakespeare."

He gave me a quick glance.

"My right good friend! I wondered why I did not see him as we came through the town. What of him?"

Then, rapidly, beseechingly, I told of his imprisonment and its cause; spoke also of Will's intention of joining the players when they came; then reached the point of my story.

"And now, wilt thou not free him?" I cried, the tears springing to my eyes unbidden, as I caught Master Burbadge's hand. "Ye are many, and the gaol

A health to—Shakespeares
freedom and—Shakes
-peares Sweetheart !

will be deserted to-morrow while the town is at the play. I will show you where the prison is. Will not some of you go and free him? Then he will to London with you, and when he comes back—ah, then the prank that made him captive may be forgotten or forgiven. O Master Burbadge, thou art his friend! Set him free, prythee set him free."

He looked at me in deep thought for an instant.

"'Tis possible, I think," he said at last, and for very joy at the words I bent and kissed his hand; "but no one must know of our plan save ourselves." He paused and looked at me as if a sudden thought had struck him. "Come," he said, and motioned to the room he had just left; "come. Thou thyself wilt be thine own best advocate."

With no thought save of Will, I followed him. The players set up a shout of joy at my entrance, but I heard them not; nor did I heed the amorous glances that some cast at me. Burbadge raised his hand to command silence.

"This maid hath a tale to tell us, my masters," he said. "Prythee listen well."

Then, quickly and to the best of my power, I told my story once again. The players were most appre-

ciative listeners. They roared with laughter at the plot against Sir Thomas, and their faces grew sober as they heard of Will's overthrow. Most of them knew him or knew of him, for many belonged to Stratford or its neighborhood; and then, he had always taken a warm interest in the players and their work. When, at length, my tale was ended and my plan to free Will was revealed, one of the actors I had not noticed before sprang upon the table, a cup of wine in his hand.

"Down with the Puritans!" he cried in a whining, nasal voice irresistibly comic. "To the rescue of gallant Will and his comrades."

"If thou shoutest out thy opinions in that fashion, Will Kempe, thou wilt join Shakespeare and his friends, instead of going to their rescue," observed Greene. "Play not the clown now. 'Tis not the time nor place!"

"Nay, chide not honest Kempe," said Burbadge, kindly, as Kempe, looking somewhat abashed, got down from the table. "He voices all our thoughts, I know. What say you, comrades? Shall we rescue Will and take him with us to London?"

"Ay," they all shouted, heartily, even Greene; while Marlowe, leaping to his feet, raised his glass in his hand as Kempe had done.

Chapter VII

 reaking the Locks of Prison Gates

The Stratford streets were deserted next day, as I passed hurriedly along them on my way to the gaol. The play was progressing in the inn-yard, and all the town, apparently, had gone thither.

Here and there an old grandsire nodded in the sun; and occasionally I saw a young mother standing in a doorway, her baby in her arms. Otherwise, all the town, young and old, rich and poor, had gone to the play.

We had counted on this condition of affairs, the players and I, when we had made our plans the day before. It cheered me now to see how aptly circumstances were falling in with our schemes. In less than a half-hour, should all go well, Will would be free.

The glad thought put a spring into my step, and I gave a low, happy laugh. At the same moment I looked up and found that I was passing Will's home, and that Mistress Shakespeare was standing by the window.

Shakespeares — Sweetheart

When I had seen her last she had carried herself in stately wise, and had looked at me with scorn and abhorrence. Now she did not see me, and her whole figure was drooping, as she leaned against the open window. One arm was curved listlessly above her head, the other rested carelessly on the sill. Her beautiful, hazel eyes, so like Will's, were wide and sad. Her exquisite, disdainful face looked pale and drawn.

My heart smote me at sight of her, so lovely and so sorrowful. Alas! what was I, to come between such a mother and such a son? Will was like her in stately figure and clear-cut features, and I could imagine how dearly they had loved each other. As I saw her drooping form, her sorrowful face, I paused involuntarily, and she glanced up and saw me. Instantly her expression hardened, and she drew herself erect.

All my impulse of pity vanished. I looked at her proudly, also. For one instant, without speaking, we faced each other thus — Shakespeare's mother and Shakespeare's sweetheart. It was the indication of our lifelong attitude. Then she vanished from the window, and I went on down the street with even, leisurely steps, my head still high in the air. A few moments later I reached the gaol.

It took hard knocking to arouse the custodian, and when he at length admitted me, he looked as if he had been sleeping.

He was grumbling to himself about his hard fate. Other men, he muttered, could go to the play; but he must remain to watch these lazy varlets who were in his charge.

"Well, here is consolation," I said, after sympathizing with his complaint. "Dame Quickly, of the inn, was once servant to the Shakespeares in their better days, and she sends a pasty to Master Will. She bade me also give this one to thee, if thou wouldst let me take his to him." This speech was a skillful mixture of fiction and fact. Dame Quickly had, indeed, been servant to the Shakespeares, but she knew nothing of the present plan.

He leered at me sleepily. "And why art thou messenger, pretty Nan?" he said, in what was intended for a fascinating manner.

I lowered my lashes as if it were indeed irresistible, and answered demurely:

"I am maid at the inn for the nonce, and Mistress Quickly was kind enough to say that she trusted me."

"Curse me, then," he cried, growing even more

sentimental, "but thou shalt do as she desires, and I will trust thee, too, on one condition. I will allow thee to take the pasty up to Will, if first thou wilt let me give thee a kiss;" and he leered at me again.

I hesitated, my face aflame. Then I laughed deprecatingly.

"Why shouldst thou care to buss me, Master?" I said. "Thou knowest me well and hast seen me oft. Why this sudden wish to touch my lips?"

"Thou hast never seemed so fair before," he answered, gazing at me amorously; "and, besides, thou art the only maid within reach. I'll have a kiss, I say, or thou shalt not take the pasty to Will Shakespeare."

His tone was growing threatening, and what mattered it, after all? A kiss was but an ordinary interchange of civilities; only I cared not to have this redfaced knave bring his face so near to mine. However, that I should reach Will speedily was of the greatest importance; and so, without more ado, I lifted my mouth to the gaoler's and gave him his desire.

"Good!" he cried, smacking his lips, after having bestowed on me several resounding kisses; "now the pasty thou didst promise me, Gramercy! Ah!" and he began to bite into it. "Mistress Quickly's hand hath

not lost its old cunning. Here are the keys, wench. I cannot leave this dainty dish."

This was more than I had hoped for. I seized the keys and fled up the stairs precipitately, leaving him busy with the pasty. I did not know in which room Will was confined, but I trusted to heaven to find out.

Meanwhile the gaoler was devouring, in huge bites, the pasty which had been drugged with a powerful liquid provided by Master Burbadge. The effect of the same would be to put him in a stupor, but it would not harm him further. So Master Burbadge assured me, or I would not have used it, even to free Will from his imprisonment.

I ran along the corridor, calling Will's name as loudly as I dared. Presently I heard his voice reply in a tone of great surprise.

Fortunately, the keys were not many, and I speedily found the one that fitted. Then, half laughing, half in tears, I stumbled into his room, to be met with a cry of utter astonishment as he caught me in his arms.

"Nan!" he cried. "Nan! whence didst thou come? What miracle is this?"

"Oh, hush!" I panted, laying my finger on his lips. "Here, here's the pasty. Thou must take it with thee

95

to avert suspicion from me. I told the players; they are coming to free thee. O Will, I had to kiss the gaoler to get to thee. There, quick! Burbadge will explain all to thee afterwards. The door is open. Come!"

"But to what end?" he began, obeying me, however, as I urged him towards the door. "Sir Thomas Lucy——"

"Thou wilt soon be far away from him," I answered, impatiently. "Come, come!"

He said no more, although he was evidently mystified, but obeyed, as I drew him with me. We ran lightly down the stairs together. The gaoler lay in a stupor, the half-eaten dainty beside him. I dropped the keys at his feet. We passed swiftly into the air, and there Master Burbadge and Master Kempe were waiting for us, according to agreement.

"Welcome, Will," cried the latter, in a voice that was no less joyous because it was in a low key from caution. "Thank this brave lass that thou art free. Art ready to go to London with us? We start within the hour, before thy gaoler shall awaken."

"I am in darkness still, although I have left my prison," answered Will, giving a hand to each of the

players as we began to walk rapidly away from the gaol, "but I think light is dawning. Ay, Burbadge, I will to London with thee, although——" he hesitated, and glanced at me.

"Fear not, Will," I interposed; "none knows of my share in thy escape save the gaoler, and methinks shame at being outwitted by a wench will keep him silent. Besides, when it is found that thou art gone with the players, they will be suspected of having set thee free. Fear not for me. To London, and god-speed!"

He stood still a moment in deep thought. Kempe looked around uneasily, but none saw us; not a soul was in sight.

"Stay," he said, suddenly; "I would first—Kempe, Burbadge, are your parts in the play over?"

"Ay," Burbadge answered; "the rest are acting the last scene now. We came to do our part in setting thee free, but find thee no longer a prisoner. What wouldst say, Will? Speak quickly, for time presses."

"How long before thou dost start for London?" said Will, who seemed curiously forgetful of his perilous position as escaped prisoner, although he walked on again in obedience to Burbadge's gesture.

97

"We have planned to do so within the hour; and so we must, if thou art to go with us, so that thy escape may not be discovered too soon."

"Then," cried Will, the light of a sudden resolve brightening his face; "I will ask one boon further, comrades. I will not join you now, but I will meet you to-morrow morn at Luddington. Go back to the players, and watch for me when you reach that town. I will join you there without fail."

"But why?" began Burbadge, expostulatingly. "'Tis foolish, needless. Why not come with us now? I have a cloak and a wig ready, which will make thee escape recognition in Stratford."

"Say what thou wilt," answered Will, obstinately. "I will join thee at Luddington, or nowhere. Ah, comrades," and his voice once more took on its usual winning quality, "believe me, I am not ungrateful. I have some business to which I must first attend, else I cannot to London with a free mind. Do as I desire, and I will meet you at Luddington."

With ill grace they consented at last and took their departure. Will seized my hand and drew me in the opposite direction. We had now nearly reached the outskirts of Stratford. "Quick, Nan," he said, "go

seek Sandells and Richardson. They dwell about a quarter of a mile further. Most like they are not at the play, since they are sober-minded men. They are faithful friends of mine, and I think will do what I ask. Bid them come with me at once and we will all to Luddington together."

"But why," I began, in utter perplexity, "why wilt thou risk thy freedom?"

Then, indeed, his face relaxed. He laughed, and kissed me.

"Dost not thou know, either?" he said, still laughing. We were now walking rapidly out of Stratford, in the opposite direction to the inn-yard, and towards the homes of Sandells and Richardson. "Because I would make thee safely my wife before I go to London, sweetheart. Now, the bans will not need to be declared, if my good friends will do as I desire. I will ask them to become sureties on a bond freeing the Bishop from liability in case of lawful impediment; which, thou knowest, does not exist. I feared lest player's bond would not suffice else would I have asked Kempe and Burbadge to do me this service. That is why I go to Luddington, sweetheart. There! yonder lies Sandells's house, and not far from it is Richard-

99

son's. Haste thee, and ask them if they will do me this favor. I will go on, since I dare not linger."

As in a dream, I obeyed him; and as in a dream, I lived during the next few hours.

Master Sandells and Master Richardson consented to Will's request, and we all made our way as quickly as possible to Luddington. There, at last, were spoken the words that made me Will's wife. In haste and secrecy our marriage took place, yet it brought us none the less joy.

The players reached Luddington that same evening, but did not depart until the following morning. Master Sandells and Master Richardson remained, also, that they might take me back to Shottery.

In the dim, chill dawn of the next day I bade Will farewell, and watched him ride away to London. All the light of my life went with him. Then, in Master Richardson and Master Sandells's kindly care, I went back to Shottery, Will's wedded wife at last, the bride of a night.

Chapter VIII

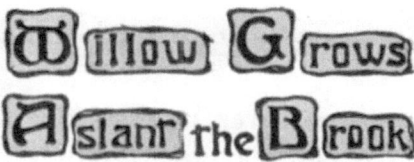

Willow Grows Aslant the Brook

Strangely, unexpectedly, my share in Will's escape remained unknown. The gaoler, as I had hoped, was ashamed of the way in which he had been outwitted; and when it was found that Will had gone with the players, the fellow did his best to make suspicion point towards them.

To do him justice, this endeavor may have arisen also from a desire to shield me. My absence from Shottery that one night was not generally known until years afterwards; for I reached home again the next morning before any was astir, and Master Sandells and Master Richardson kept faith. Altogether, I was shielded in a way I scarce had dared to expect; and the months that followed Will's departure, although dull, were not unhappy. It was for his good that we were separated. I was his true wife. I had his letters to cheer me. What more could I desire at present?

Sir Thomas stormed and raged, indeed, when he found that his chief prisoner had escaped; but public

sentiment was against him, and he dared not go too far. The players were under powerful protection, and he did not wish to meet a rebuff in an attempt to get Will back. So gradually all became calm once more. The other lads were released, one by one; and at last the deer-stealing episode was almost forgotten.

There followed then, after that expedition to Charlcote and the events connected with it, a peaceful, monotonous year. Will's letters often brightened it; he came once or twice to see me, secretly, since Sir Thomas's wrath had not then died away; and before its close there was set upon my brows the crown of a woman's life.

My babe, Susannah, was born. She was a sturdy lass, with Will's chestnut hair and my dark eyes, and it seemed to me that a sweeter, prettier infant never lived. Will's delight when he heard of her birth overflowed into a letter so full of the perfect bliss and pride of fatherhood that I have long since destroyed it, deeming it too sacred to be read by other eyes. He longed to come to the christening, but could not, being detained in London; and he did not see the little lass for many weary months.

Ah, how the gossips' tongues clacked when Su-

sannah was born! Our marriage still remained secret, and I think the impression never quite died away in Stratford, even after all was known, that the little lass was a nameless child, as her mother had been. For me, I cared not. Safe in the harbor of Will's honorable love, I could wait to let time justify us both. Master Sandells and Master Richardson came to me, when the gossip reached their ears, and asked me whether they should keep silence still. I answered, proudly, ay, nor did I ever regret it. I was accustomed to averted glances and looks askance. They could not harm me, while I knew the truth. Will would have been vexed had he been aware of the state of affairs; but as I alone was concerned, I chose to suit myself. I was too proud to offer justification. 'Twas a mistake, perhaps, yet I do not regret it, even now.

Meanwhile Will's letters spoke of increasing success, of growing popularity, whereat my heart rejoiced. He had not as yet written a play, but he had helped to remodel old ones, and had acted in very many. His prospects seemed fair, and I was glad. Soothly, ay, that year was not unhappy; in the light of what followed it stands out bright and blessed.

And now, at last, I come to the place in my story

where I must, as it were, begin to write with my heart's blood. Alack! alack! how anguished is e'en the memory of that awful time! Yet it must be told, to make my tale complete. One confusion of horror and perplexity it is in the recollection; yet I must e'en disentangle the snarled threads and tell all as it happened, so far as may be.

One fair autumn day I took my little Susannah with me into Stratford. She was now several months old, and an adorable babe, full of pretty pranks and charming rogueries. I had some message to Mistress Quickly from my grandam, and I took Susannah with me, partly because I could never bear to have her far from my sight and also because she was a favorite with good Dame Quickly.

As usual, I had a pleasant time with the mistress at the inn, while Susannah was petted and fussed over to her heart's content. Dame Quickly had been a loyal friend to me during the past year, and this kindness I had never forgotten. My business ended, at length, I left her, and my babe and I went down for a brief stroll beside the willows on the river's bank before returning to Shottery. Susannah loved the sweeping, graceful trees, and she laughed and crowed, and

willow grows aslant
the brook

stretched her dimpled hands towards them in high glee.

We were very happy. Only Will's presence was needed to make our happiness complete. I told my babe so, talking to her in the fond, foolish way that mothers have. We were seated beside the stream as I said it, Susannah at play on my knees; and as I caught her closer to my heart at the thought of her dear father, behold, I heard his name!

"Will Shakespeare!" said a woman's full, rich voice in a tone of contempt. "Will Shakespeare!"

The words came from a point near by. I was sitting close to the bank of the stream, quite hidden on each side by the low, sweeping branches of the willows. Cautiously I crept back a space and peeped around the tree to see who had spoken.

These were no Stratford folk who sat there by the Avon, both brave in silks and jewels. Upon the ground the man had spread his yellow satin cloak, and beside it he half knelt, half reclined. Upon this glowing throne there sat, with regal air, the most beauteous and the most haughty woman mine eyes have e'er beheld; soothly, a queen in seeming.

I saw her afterwards many times; and to my mem-

107

ory of her then is doubtless added succeeding recollec-
tions. Yet never was her scornful loveliness so vivid
and so perfect in my sight as that first time I beheld it.

She was very dark, gloriously, ominously dark.
Her raven hair was lustreless, a cloudy background to
her perfect face. Deep blue were her eyes, of the color
that grows black in excitement or in passion. They
were almond-shaped, and heavily fringed with dark,
curling lashes. Her nose was straight, with quivering,
scornful nostrils; and no words of mine could convey
the haughty sweetness of that mouth like Cupid's bow.

Her skin was clear and smooth, and I could see
that the rich color mantling upon it was due to no
cosmetic. For the rest, her figure was all voluptuous,
sweeping curves, set off by the close-fitting crimson
taffeta she wore, and the rubies at her throat, upon her
hands.

Her companion I did not note at once. He was
in court attire, his colors blue and gold, and he had
yellow, curling hair and a chestnut beard. So much
I saw in a rapid, fleeting glance, and then my eyes
turned once more in fascination to the wondrous face
beside him. As I looked, she spoke again, in that
strangely rich, melodious voice.

"Will Shakespeare!" she exclaimed again, more petulantly this time. "Thou dost ring the changes on his name until I am right weary of the sound. Dost think I would stoop to favor a mere player?"

Her companion shrugged his shoulders and raised his eyebrows. Yet methought he looked at her in somewhat anxious wise.

"None may dare predict aught about thee, Countess," he said, half mockingly, yet with a singular deference.

She gave him a side glance from under her sweeping lashes.

"Nay, thou didst not foresee," she observed, with a little laugh, "thou didst not foresee when thou didst present Will Shakespeare to me that within one short fortnight he would be my slave."

I did not hear the other's reply to that taunting little speech. The words had gone as a dagger to mine own heart. I started involuntarily, and the babe Susannah, in my arms, opened her mouth to give a frightened cry. I laid my hand fiercely across her lips. At that moment, rather than be discovered before I heard more, methinks I could have stilled forever her baby breath.

109

For an instant pain and passion made me blind and deaf to all about me. When I could see and hear again the woman was speaking.

" 'For what is life?' Will Shakespeare said to me; 'what is life without love; love such as you can bestow, madam, and only you?' Poor fellow! He pleaded well, and seemed passion-shaked indeed. But I——" she flung out her white hands with a gesture of abandon; "I have sworn that in love matters I shall never be the conquered, but the conqueror!"

The man sighed, and for an instant turned his face thoughtfully towards the gentle stream flowing past so placidly. Only for a second stayed he so, however. No man near that face and figure could gaze long elsewhere than upon them.

"Thou art playing with a noble heart, madam," he said, gravely.

She laughed; and the sound was a very ripple of concentrated scorn.

"Say'st thou so? Well, I know not, my Lord William. Soothly, methinks 'tis because his name and thine are the same that thou art so leal a friend to him. But," she leaned towards him with an air of mystery, "but know'st thou what gossip I heard the other

day? Dame Rumor saith it that my handsome player hath already a sweetheart here in Stratford town."

I did not start again, but a shudder ran through me. Who was this woman who had discovered Will's love and mine, and why was she in Stratford now?

"Kit Marlowe, in his cups, betrayed the secret," the Countess went on, carelessly. "Whether the tale be true I know not, but sooth, if it be so——"

She came to a long pause, and for the first time her wondrous face was in repose. She sat gazing at the Avon, as he had done a moment since, and her eyes were large and dark.

"If it be true," she repeated presently, and as she spoke her mocking expression returned, "his is no noble soul, but that of a false coward; for the tale goes further, that there is a child, also. And after that, he comes——" she made a gesture of contempt and abruptly changed her sentence; "he is as other men— as thou art, for example."

He started at the words, and seized her hand beseechingly. She made no attempt to withdraw it, but let it stay passively within his grasp. It was as if she felt so remote from him in spirit that the enforced imprisonment of her hand was a matter of little moment.

"'As other men,'" he repeated, in a voice hoarse with feeling. "Nay, that am I not, dear heart; beloved! Thou knowest that thy words are untrue. I have no desire to use thee as the toy of an idle hour; nor are any of my professions of dishonorable intent. To-morrow, to-day, would I wed thee, if thou wouldst consent. Goddess of my idolatry, saint of my prayers——"

She interrupted him at this point with another short, scornful laugh. Her hand she withdrew from his, and patted him on the cheek with a certain contempt.

"Child, child, thrice a child, though grown to man's estate!" she exclaimed in a voice full of mirth, yet methought also with a hint of pain. "No saint am I, nor ever shall be. Even a fond man's blasphemy cannot make me so. Cease raving, William, and let us go back for the horses. My Lord of Leicester will miss our presence at Kenilworth."

With a face of deep dejection he offered his hand to assist her to rise. She sprang gracefully to her feet without his aid, and moved to depart, her lithe, supple figure, with its perfect curves, showing clearly against the green of the meadow. He stooped, lifted the cloak, and threw it carelessly over his arm.

"One moment, Countess," he said, speaking suddenly, as if unable to restrain himself; "wilt not tell me now why it was thy whim to ride hither?"

"Canst not guess?" she answered, and shook her finger at him. "Oh, stupid man! Being so near, I was curious to behold what kind of town it was in which thy paragon was reared, and moreover—well, I wish to find out whether Kit Marlowe's tale be very sooth, and whether thine idol may still remain on his pedestal. Come, let us to the inn. The dame there seems a garrulous mistress. We can find out from her what we desire to know."

"Why dost wish to find out?" he said, doggedly, still not moving; and my own heart echoed his question.

Again she gave him that dangerous side glance from under her long lashes.

"That, my lord," she observed, with a touch of hauteur, "that concerns me alone. Wilt go to the inn with me? If not, I will seek it myself;" and again she moved a pace or two.

He followed her, of course, and they walked slowly away, without either having discovered my presence. I watched them until the last glimpse of blue and

crimson had vanished from my sight. Then I turned, and, clutching my child to my breast, gazed out tragically at the placid Avon. Susannah had fallen asleep. How long I stood thus, what mad thoughts of a swift death beneath the smiling water tormented me I can scarce say. My mind was in a turmoil. My next clear recollection is of sinking to the ground and bursting into a passion of tears. My child awoke and cried, also, and so we crouched and sobbed there by the willows, a forlorn pair enough, while the autumn leaves fell softly about us.

Heedless of the flight of time in my dumb misery, I know not how long it was before I saw the twilight beginning to descend. I welcomed the darkness as a friend. A few hours since I would have dreaded traversing the road to Shottery alone at night. Now the dusk would serve as a mask to screen my distress from curious eyes.

By this time the haughty Countess and her attendant knight would have satisfied their curiosity. They would know me for what I was, forlorn and deserted. My tears were gone now. I was past weeping. With a long sigh I lifted Susannah to my bosom.

"Come, Sue, come little one," I said, aloud; and

wearily I noted the dull sadness of my voice; "we must home to grandam, our only friend now, sweeting, our only friend. Thy father is dead, my baby; dead, and he never saw thee; and thy mother's heart is broken, little love!"

Chapter IX

Slowly and painfully I walked back to Shottery that evening, holding my fretful babe to my bosom. I met no one as I went, but at the door of the cottage my grandam stood, anxiously awaiting me. I remember her shocked exclamation when she saw my face in the light, and I recollect how I put Susannah into her arms with a smile which must have been ghastly, indeed, and said:

"She is thine, now, grandam. Poor little orphan! Her father and mother are dead!"

And at that the color fled from my face, and I dropped prone across the threshold.

With that swoon a long blank in my memory begins. This part of my story must be written entirely from what my grandam and others have told me since. I recollect nothing from the time I dropped unconscious on the floor of our cottage until a later day, months afterwards, of which I shall speak in due course.

My grandam, in alarm and perplexity, strove at

once to restore me; but the attempt was vain for some time. The babe was wailing piteously from fright and hunger, and my grandam at length turned her attention to Susannah, soothed her with difficulty, and at last laid her to rest. When my grandam returned she was surprised to find me risen to a sitting position.

"So thou art better, Nan," she said, in a relieved way, as she hastened towards me. I turned and looked at her with blank, unseeing eyes.

"Better?" I repeated, in a toneless voice. "Nay, I shall never be better. My heart is broken, grandam, broken, I tell thee——" I leaned towards her, coaxingly, and caught her hands in mine.

"Send word to Will, and he'll come," I whispered. "He will come and cure me." Then a sudden convulsion crossed my face and I flung her hands away. "Nay, nay!" I cried, wildly. "I had forgot. He will never come again; no, no, no, never again!" and with tears in mine eyes I crooned a snatch of an old country song:

"Will he not come again,
Will he not come again?
No, no, he is dead;
Gone to his death-bed;
He never will come again!"

120

My grandam stood an instant in stony silence, while I rocked and muttered before the fire. Past and present seemed to meet as she gazed at me. Often had she seen my mother thus, gloomy and distraught. Was the long nightmare of her life to be repeated in her child?

"Nay, Nan," she said at length, coaxingly; "nay, Nan, thou art mistaken. He will come again surely, lass, and bring joy to thee and me. To bed now. Little Sue is already sleeping."

She attempted to lift me; but I withstood her, pettishly. "Let be, let be," I muttered, gazing into the fire and pointing to the red embers. "I am watching the autumn leaves. Once they were green, and tender and young. It was May then. What comes in May? Ah, yes, I remember; it is love!

> " 'It was a lover and his lass,
>   Sing hey and ho, and ho nonnino!
>   And through the green fields they did pass,
>   In the spring time——'

"But 'tis autumn. Crimson are they, those leaves, like the blood of my heart. My heart is broken and I am dead. Why am I not buried, grandam?"

"Thou dreamest, Nan," said my grandam, but her voice was hopeless.

"Ah, I know," I murmured, wisely, nodding at the fire. " 'Tis because there are no violets. I must have violets upon my grave. Canst not get me some, grandam? Then I could rest; and I am tired, oh, so tired!" I moved my head restlessly from side to side, and moaned.

"Child, they are all withered," my grandam answered, attempting to humor my fancy.

"Ay, I know," I answered, instantly. " 'Twas when Will died that they withered, was't not? Methinks he died in autumn; I cannot remember——

> " 'They bore him barefaced on his bier,
> And on his grave rained many a tear.'

"Nay, I cannot remember—I must be patient.

> " 'It is my lady! oh, it is my love!'

"So spake he, but I bade him swear not by the moon, because it changes oft. He must have done so, after all. And yet——

> " 'Bonny sweet Robin is all my joy!'

122

"Nay, that is wrong. Robin is not the name. 'Tis —'tis—ah, yes! I know; 'tis Will!"

With that I sprang up suddenly, with a joyous laugh, and went to the door. My grandam interposed before I could open it.

"Where art going, lass?" she said, soothingly. " 'Tis late, dear maid."

"Will comes late," I answered, with a happy smile. "The world does not know yet, but he is mine. The moon has risen. He will be here soon. Let me go, grandam. I must to the gate to meet him. Let me go, I say!" I narrowed my eyes and looked at her in threatening wise. She deemed it best to give me my way, and stood aside. I flung wide the door and looked out.

The beauteous afternoon had ended in a dreary night. Rain was beginning to fall. The sky was pitchy dark. The path to the gate was strewn thick with autumn leaves. A dreary wind was howling.

For an instant I stood gazing at the dismal scene, with mute but increasing distress. Then I turned and fell sobbing into my grandam's arms; weeping, I allowed her to lead me to bed; tearfully, I let her do with me as she would. And I was tractable for the remainder of that night.

She had some hope that when morning came I would be restored to my usual state; but it was not so to be. My first waking, troubled words referred again to Will's death, to faded violets, and to some crimson horror which apparently preyed upon my mind. My poor grandam was in dire perplexity and distress as regarded my wanderings. She had no clue to the mystery. In the morning she brought the babe Susannah to me, trusting that I would be aroused at sight of her. Instead, I looked at the child with lack-lustre eyes, although the dear poppet crowed and stretched out her dimpled hands to me. Then suddenly I began to weep again, and to murmur sorrowful words about her orphaned state.

That was the beginning of a weary winter, the most sorrowful one of my grandam's sad life. She knew of absolutely no reason for my condition. I had mentioned Mistress Quickly's name in my wanderings, and my grandam went to consult her, but was not aided thereby. The cheery innkeeper did not connect me with the fine visitors she had had. As I learned long afterwards, the Countess and Lord William had made their inquiries with seeming carelessness, and had not dwelt long upon the subject. Neither Mistress Quickly

nor my grandam suspected that their presence in Stratford was responsible for my condition.

My grandam could neither read nor write; so she had no way of letting Will know about my state. Letters came from him occasionally, but they were as a sealed book to her. Afterwards I read these, and found that they gradually grew more wondering and insistent as to the cause of my silence. He wrote that he could not well leave London during the winter, but when spring came he would seek Stratford speedily. Meanwhile, why, why did I not write?

Once or twice my grandam thought of asking someone to write to Will; but she was a proud woman, and she felt, from what I said in my wanderings, that something must be wrong between us; that he was, in some mysterious way, partly responsible for my condition, and all her old mistrust of him revived.

The poor babe felt the change in her mother; and from a healthy, happy child, turned into a quiet, pensive infant. My grandam oft hath said since that it was sad to see how little Sue would sit and gaze at me in mournful silence, as if half-comprehending that something was wrong. As for me, I took no notice whatever of the babe. It was as if she did not exist.

Wearily, sadly, the months dragged away, until at last the spring-time came. With the violets for which I had longed, my healing seemed to begin. I grew less gloomy. I loved to be out of doors, and to deck myself with flowers. I began to notice the child, and to play with her a little. My grandam saw these happy changes, and, almost unbidden, hope sprang up again in her heart.

The final restoration of my wits came at length, without warning. One balmy day in early April I came in from the fields, crowned and garlanded with flowers. I sang snatches of old songs and murmured about the same old themes. The next morning I awoke myself again, the past months a blank, the afternoon beneath the willows alone a distinct remembrance.

Never did I see my grandam so moved as when she found, that day, that I was once more myself. She gazed at me a moment, I remember, with incredulous joy. Then as I made some sensible remarks about the babe at play near by, she suddenly burst into tears.

"Anne, Anne," she cried, coming close to me and looking yearningly into my face; "is it truly thou thyself once more?" And then she checked her words, as I gazed at her in amazement.

126

"Why not, dear grandam?" I said, wonderingly, looking at her with inquiring glance. "Ah!" and my face clouded; "thou meanest that conversation that so troubled me. Sooth, it brought me much sadness; but I have thought it over, and meseems that perhaps—— Well, we will talk later about that. Where is the babe? Come hither, sweet, and kiss thy mother."

A short time after, I told her, apparently with little emotion, of the words I had overheard by the willows that autumn day. To my listener it made many more things clear than I quite understood then. I remember still the anxious feeling I had while narrating the incident. It was as if what I told was about some other person, for whom I felt sorry. When I had finished, I added, in a business-like way:

"It would not be fair to Will, I have concluded, to take their word, without having seen with mine own eyes whether they spoke truth. I will to London and find out for myself."

My grandam stared at me aghast. I spoke as airily as if going to London were as easy an affair as walking into Stratford. She did not venture to cross me, however; but, hoping to divert my attention from the idea I had just expressed, she brought out Will's

127

letters and gave them to me without comment. Her
wish was that my desire to go to him would vanish
when I had learned the contents of the letters; but
she was disappointed.

I opened the epistles and read them calmly. They
did not arouse any wonder in my mind; why, I have
never been able to understand. I was not impressed
by the number of the letters, nor by the change in tone
of their contents. The first few were simply narratives
of events; but as time had gone on, and he had still
not heard from me, the spirit of the epistles had grown
first wondering, then reproachful. The last one vowed
that if I did not write within a month he would run
down to Stratford to find the cause of my long silence.
He added that he had been sore distressed throughout
the winter, owing to the lack of news from Shottery;
but his business had held him close in London.

I pondered over this last letter with something like
a sneer. If, indeed, the words of the Countess were
true, his duties had soothly held him close in London;
and if so—— I went to the window and looked out.
Beyond I saw the fair familiar scene in its spring freshness and beauty. When I had gazed thence last, con-
sciously, it had lain in autumn desolation.

"It is spring," I said, turning at last to my grandam, with a sudden smile; "spring, and the roads are open. Within a fortnight I ride to London, grandam."

"But, lass," she answered, cautiously, scarce knowing what to say, "I fear me that thou canst not. The way to London is long and hard. For a man, even, 'tis difficult; for a woman, impossible."

I broke into light laughter, ran over to her and threw both my arms around her neck. She stared at me uneasily. Such demonstration was new on my part.

"Ay," I cried, gayly; "ay, thou'rt right. Impossible for a woman, thou say'st sooth; but for a man, grandam; even a young one; a mere boy——" I paused and smiled at her in mocking, suggestive fashion.

"Nan, what mean'st thou?" said my grandam, startled into sternness. She feared that my wits had once more gone wandering; and I am not sure now but that they were; "what mean'st thou, lass?"

I laughed again, and leaned my cheek against hers.

"A doublet and hose, a cloak," I whispered; "these would transform any woman. Moreover, dyed hair, and skin stained dark—dost think e'en a lover would know his mistress thus, much less a husband—faith-

less perchance?" My face grew dark for an instant, then lighted with laughter again.

"Ay, for a woman 'tis nigh impossible to travel to London; but for a boy, e'en one so slight as I— what think'st thou, grandam?"

I released her and laughed again. Then I stuck my hand upon my hip in jaunty boyish fashion, and strode up and down the room, humming an air in braggadocio-wise.

My grandam sat gazing at me helplessly. She knew my meaning now. Madder than ever was I, she had no doubt; and yet how dared she cross me?

Chapter X

 Pretty Boy

 A fortnight later, as I had planned, I joined a party at a near-by town and started out for London. My grandam had yielded to me in sheer despair. Soothly, I think she deemed my wits still wandering. Belike, they were, after a fashion.

Looking back, methinks 'twas the last remnant of my madness that made me so bold to devise, so determined in execution. Many of the players had seen me before, and this made recognition possible. Therefore, I stained my skin and dyed my close-cropped hair. The male attire was a difficulty, but my grandam measured me and took the items to a tailor in a town near by. The suit he sent home fitted me ill, but served my purpose. Should any ask the cause of my absence, in Stratford or in Shottery, my grandam was to say that I had gone to spend some time with a cousin in a distant town. She trusted, so she was to add, that change of air and scene would restore my bewildered senses.

With what dire misgivings, with how foreboding

133

a heart, my grandam saw me begin that journey to London I can only partly conjecture. It was in the early dawn that I left the cottage door, with never a glance backward at her standing with the babe in the doorway. I seemed to be possessed with but one thought, to go to London and to Will, and learn whether the tale I had heard were calumny or truth. I had no place in my mind for any other person or idea.

That journey is not clear in my remembrance. It presented fewer difficulties than I had expected; for I was a country lass, accustomed to rough roads and bluff companions. I was used to walking, yet could ride, if occasion required. My purse was not deep, but it was by no means empty. I did not suffer hunger at any time, nor extreme fatigue, and I met many kindnesses along the way. I suppose I looked so boyish and so young that men and women both strove to treat me gently. Many a good housewife gave me a meal and scoffed at the idea of payment. Many a pretty girl looked softly upon me and offered me fruit or flowers, with no recompense but a kiss. Burly men, thinking perhaps of a young son at home, befriended me, also, while lads of my own apparent age adopted me as comrade. Altogether my journey to London

proved to me that the world was a less cruel place than I had deemed it on that autumn afternoon by the willows.

At last, one fair spring morn, we rode into London. As we entered the city the mists and shadows that had obscured my brain seemed suddenly to clear away. It was as if, my goal attained, the thorny way that I had trodden was forgot. Near the haven of my desire, my stormy voyage thither dwelt no longer in my remembrance. So, perhaps, after life's trials and sorrows, the blessed feel who rest within the gates of Paradise.

Soothly, like Paradise, indeed, looked to me those green gardens and fair mansions past which I rode that spring morning. The thought crossed my mind that Will would not have far to go to renew the remembrances of his country home. Here, as in Stratford, on the outskirts of the city, were woods and winding streams. Here, as there, rose homes quaint and stately, surrounded by beauteous gardens. Even after we entered London proper we still saw many green lawns and budding flowers, and heard the birds singing joyously among the trees.

At length, after one or two inquiries on my part, I safely reached the precinct of St. Helen's, where I

135

knew Will's lodgings lay. Instinctively, I sought the nearest inn, thinking to ask there more particularly as to his accustomed haunts.

The place was dark and low-ceiled, and as I entered it I blinked and saw little until my eyes became accustomed to the subdued light. When, finally, I was able to distinguish my surroundings, I gave a slight start. The room was empty save for one group around a table just across from me. In that cluster of faces there were four out of the half-dozen that I knew; one of them my heart leapt to behold. Marlowe sat there, with his handsome, dissipated face and wild, sparkling eyes. Burbadge was gazing at the others with his accustomed meditative look. A scowl, as usual, spoiled Greene's fair, boyish face. Talking eagerly, persuasively, Will stood back of Marlowe's chair, but his voice was too low for me to catch his words.

The other two members of the group were strange to me. One, I was afterwards to learn, was Master Jonson, at that time just beginning his career. He was short and rather stout, with a kindly, wise face that I learned later to love well. I have said that he was stout; yet he appeared not so that afternoon. His bulk faded into insignificance because placed beside a very

136

mountain of flesh. To his right, looking over the table, sat a fellow so fat that he filled the places of three ordinary men. At first sight he was disgusting in his tremendous size; but there was a droll expression in his rubicund face which promised more value in his society than his general appearance indicated.

My back was towards the light, and although they all gave me a quick glance as I entered, their gaze did not rest on me for any length of time. With an odd feeling, between relief and disappointment at their lack of recognition, I found a place, still carefully keeping my back to the window, and ordered wine. The group around the table, having seen, apparently, but a slender country lad, continued their conversation freely.

Will went on speaking rapidly for a few minutes; but I could not understand what he said. Then I heard Robin Greene's high, petulant voice in reply.

"Say what thou wilt, I'll not; and there's an end," he said, positively and disagreeably.

Will became suddenly silent. He possessed the rare talent of knowing when words are useless. Marlowe grimaced at Greene and gave an expressive shrug. Burbadge looked troubled, and Jonson meditative. The fat man suddenly broke the silence.

137

"Think again, Robin, sweet wag," he said, and the coaxing tones of his oily voice were almost irresistibly wheedling. "'Tis always well to oblige a friend; Will is thy friend; therefore——"

"Thy idea of a friend is one who pays the tavern reckoning, as Will hath done to-day," observed Burbadge, somewhat dryly.

The fat man looked at him with gentle reproach.

"Well, so thou say'st," he said, heaving a great sigh that almost made the table shake; "thou say'st—it may be true. God forgive ye, lads, 'tis your fault if so it be. Before I knew the players I knew nothing evil."

He sighed again as they gave a derisive shout of laughter; but there was a twinkle in his eyes.

"Why, thou old sinner!" cried Marlowe, clapping him on the back; "'tis thou that leadest us astray. If there be any scandal in London, who hath it at his tongue's end? Jack! If there be a lady to serenade, or a purse to steal, who is ready for either? Jack! Sooth, now I bethink me, thou didst escape hardly from that last adventure of thine upon the highway." He winked at the others. "Tell us about it, Jack."

The fat man cleared his throat impressively, and

a look of extreme gravity and importance came upon his face. The eyes of the rest grew merry, and they crowded as closely about him as his bulk permitted.

"'Twas at Eastcheap, one dark night, a month since," he began with unction.

"Methought 'twas in Blackfriars a year ago," murmured Marlowe, with mock interest.

"Nay, thou art mistaken," replied the fat man, gravely; "'twas as I have stated but now."

"It boots not," said Will, with extreme politeness, his eyes bright with amusement. "Proceed, Sir John!"

"Sir John!" exclaimed the stout story-teller in a gratified tone. "Ah, Will, good friend, thou art the only one who so calls me; yet truly I deserve a title, for I have done valorous deeds in my time. Not the first is this I am about to tell thee of. It happened near the theatre, across the river."

"Nay, 'twas at Eastcheap," said Burbadge, laughingly. Jack gazed at him reproachfully.

"Thou must have misunderstood me strangely," he said in a tone of mild correction. "'Twas in Blackfriars that it chanced——"

"What?" interrupted Robin Greene, petulantly; "that what chanced?"

139

"This of which I am about to tell thee," answered Sir John, imperturbably. There was a laugh at Greene's expense, and he subsided, frowning. The fat man paused to drink a measure of wine; then continued, impressively:

"By a dozen was I beset that night, and for two hours together did I engage with them. Eight times was I thrust through the doublet, and four through the hose, my buckler cut through and through, my sword hacked like a hand saw——"

"Sooth, no hero of Troy knew ever such a combat," observed Jonson, wiping his eyes, which were filled with tears of laughter.

"How didst thou live?" asked Marlowe, with mock horror.

"Heroes are not as other men," said Will, gravely. His eyes were very bright, and they were fixed on Sir John. "Proceed, proceed!"

"Ay," continued the fat man, growing excited as he went on, and rising ponderously to act out his story; "sixteen, at least, set upon me that night. Sixteen, said I? Nay, fifty. Beshrew me if there were not two or three and fifty upon poor old Jack! Two of them I peppered well;" he drew his sword and flourished

140

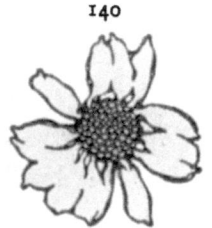

it in the air; "thus I bore my point. Four rogues in buckram then let drive at me——"

"Two," interjected Greene, quickly.

"Four, little Rob," returned Sir John, gazing at him in a paternal manner that immediately reduced Greene to voiceless rage. "All their seven points I took in my target thus." He illustrated dramatically.

"Seven? O Jack, Jack!" cried Marlowe, with a roar of laughter.

"Seven, by these hilts," replied Sir John in a solemn, offended tone. "These nine in buckram then began to give me ground; but seven of the eleven I paid——"

"Enough!" cried Jonson, laughing heartily. "Homer and Virgil are quite surpassed, and the tragic heroes of Rome and Greece are as naught beside thee and thy deeds, Sir John."

Sir John bowed and smiled, with a look of gratified vanity.

"Of none of them can it be said," cried Greene, rudely, striking the sword out of the fat man's hand with a deft turn of his own wrist; "of none of them can it be said that they fought eleven buckram men grown out of two!"

At the insulting words and action the fat man's face became furious. By a dexterous movement, singular in one of his size, he recovered his sword, and with the flat of it began to belabor Greene over the shoulders.

"Thou boy, thou cur, thou pig!" he cried between the strokes. "Thou art beneath aught but chastisement, else would I demand the satisfaction of a gentleman; and I would prove to thee my swordsmanship, thou——"

"Peace, peace," interrupted Will, arresting Sir John's sword at imminent danger of its being turned upon himself, and motioning the fat man to his seat. "Robin is but a lad, Sir John; forgive him. Robin, thou dost not well to doubt the knight's word. Come, landlord, another cup of sack!"

With some difficulty the storm was calmed; Sir John, breathing forth threatenings against Robin Greene, at length subsided into his former place. His tormentor and victim, almost weeping with pain and rage, shook his boyish fists at the fat man, in impotent anger. Marlowe sat laughing derisively at them both, but Burbadge's face remained grave. Jonson was pouring forth a flood of classical comparisons, in which

the late undignified encounter was likened to some of
the famous combats before Troy. Will's face wore an
abstracted expression. Meseemed he looked older and
graver than when I had seen him last. At length all
became peaceful again. Sir John, having gulped down
much liquor, presently nodded himself into a doze.
Greene sat in sulky silence. The rest became quiet
when the fat man's inspiring jollity had sunk into
slumber.

"The old villain!" said Marlowe, gazing at him
contemplatively. "He's rare sport, indeed, but what a
liar! Thy mock title soothly delights him greatly,
Will. 'Tis said there's some strain of noble blood in
him, which accounts for his pleasure when thou dost
dub him knight. Why dost humor him so?"

Will smiled a little, but made no reply.

"Canst not conjecture, Marlowe?" interposed Burbadge, quickly and kindly. "Sir John will be in a play
some day that will capture the town. Then the Queen's
Majesty——"

Will interrupted him by a gesture of protest.

"Castles in Spain," he said, lightly, yet methought
somewhat sadly, also. "Castles in Spain! Sooth, such
are they like to remain, meseems just now—Robin,

Robin, thou knowest my future welfare may hang on this performance. Wilt not act my Juliet?"

"Nay," said Robin, curtly and decisively, and turned his back upon the others.

"Thou saucy lad!" began Jonson, angrily.

"Thy reason?" said Burbadge, gazing at the boy sternly. He pouted and shrugged his shoulders, but made no other reply.

"He's the only player who will look the part," said Jonson, mournfully. A fleeting glance of triumph swept over Greene's face at the words.

Burbadge sighed and looked away from the rest in thought. As he did so his eyes fell on me. His face brightened a little and he touched Will's arm and whispered in his ear.

Fully conscious of his movement, yet obliged to appear unseeing, I sat in agony for a moment. Was I recognized, in this place, among this company? A strange feeling, half joy, half sorrow, tugged at my heart. The next instant I was calm again. At Burbadge's whispered words Will uttered an exclamation of relief. He rose and came towards me. The rest stared at him in amazement; then, with one accord, followed, all except Greene and Sir John. The group

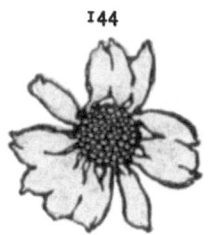

closed around the table where I sat. There was no recognition in their gaze. Even Will looked me in the eyes and knew me not.

He spoke presently with the ready charm that was always his.

"Good-morrow, lad. Hast come to London to seek thy fortune? By thy countenance and dress I judge that thou art not of the city."

I nodded, my eyes searching his face half eagerly, half fearfully, for any sign of recognition. I did not find it.

"Why, then, thy fortune's thine without seeking further," Will continued, cheerily. "We're players, lad. Wilt join us? Thy face and figure are rarely suited to a woman's part, and lads like thee are scarce in London town. Yon fellow, sulking at the table, hath been the only one, and he is spoilt through prosperity. Wilt be his rival?"

I looked at the different players, hesitating, dubious. I had not dreamed of this; yet in what better way could my mission be accomplished? Will thought my silence rose from boyish timidity, and continued, kindly, encouragingly.

"I have a play, an Italian play, and need a heroine

145

for it." He looked at me critically again, and murmured:

"It is my lady; oh, it is my love!"

I had to hold myself rigid to prevent a visible shiver running through me. Alack! what bitter-sweet memories those words awakened!

At that moment Robin Greene awoke to some inkling of what was going on. He rose from the table and joined the rest.

"Who is this?" he said in his high-pitched voice, gazing at me superciliously.

"Thy rival, Robin!" cried Marlowe, with a great laugh, as he clapped him on the shoulder.

A mean, dangerous expression came into Greene's eyes. He looked at me jealously, contemptuously; then darted a glance of hatred at Will. The last look decided me.

"I am at your service, sirs," I said, speaking in a voice higher than my natural one, in order to disguise it more effectually. "I will follow you, master," I said to Will. And thus quickly my mission was half-performed.

Jonson's face and Burbadge's lighted generously.

146

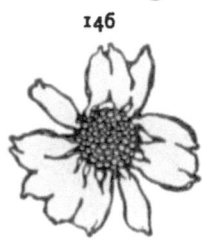

Marlowe gazed from Greene's jealous countenance to mine with a look of malicious amusement.

Will's face relaxed, and he smiled the rare and tender smile that I had once loved well.

"Then welcome, my Juliet," said he, and gave me his hand to seal the compact.

Chapter XI

 **Dark Lady** ❦

One fair June day, a few weeks after that scene in the tavern, I stood at the entrance of the Globe, idly awaiting a rehearsal. So far, most of my plans had been carried out with a success beyond my most hopeful dreams. I had obtained confidential access to Will without the least difficulty. I was with him every day, my lodgings were near his, we talked and worked together; yet he showed no passing realization of my identity.

I had displaced Robin Greene in Will's new play, thereby making the former the lasting enemy of us both. I had become a favorite among the actors in general, however, and they made much of me. The stout Sir John patronized me with his usual humorous effrontery. Marlowe was contemptuously kind. He knew not how to show good feeling otherwise. Jonson treated me in hearty, whole-souled fashion, while Burbadge was fatherly and courteous, as was his wont towards all things young and delicate. The rest were kindly, too; I was their friend and confidant. I heard

all the gossip of the company; their loves and hates, their sins and virtues; yet——

I passed my hand across my brow with an impatient gesture as the thought came to me, as often before, that June morning. I had been told the faults and foibles, the weaknesses and transgressions, of so many in the company. And yet—not one had mentioned the Countess, nor had any spoken of him she had called Lord William that afternoon beside the Avon. Could it be that they both had lied? If so, why the falsehood, since they thought none was by to hear? If their words had been truth, why had none of the players mentioned the existence of either Count or Countess? To be sure, they had been busy with the new play; still——

I was waiting now for Will, who, as usual, was to direct the rehearsal that morning. He was later than was his custom, since he had said the day before that he expected to bring a friend with him to rehearsal. When he had so spoken the others had looked at each other significantly. I had caught their quick glances, and had wondered as to their meaning.

Suddenly, as I stood there, impatiently awaiting Will's coming, I saw a small boat leave the opposite

shore and move rapidly in the direction of the Globe. As the tiny craft drew near I saw that there were two occupants besides the boatman. One was Will; the other——

Involuntarily I put both hands over my heart, as if to hush its wild beating. I closed my eyes dizzily for a moment, then opened them and stared again at Will's companion. I had seen, before, that handsome, careless face, and the stately figure in its bravery of blue and gold. The yellow cloak, glistening in the sunlight, I had beheld spread as a throne for her who had wrecked my life, the dark enchantress who had lured my love from me. Was my mission to London nearly completed, was my problem almost solved?

Fortunately, no one was near to witness my agitation, and by the time the boat had landed I had regained my self-possession. Will and the Count sprang to the shore and came towards me in confidential conversation with each other. The Count paused to throw a coin to the boatman. It glistened yellow in the sun.

"There!" he cried; "there's for thy pains, good fellow! Take it as token of my joy to be once more in London with my good comrade," and again he passed his arm affectionately across Will's shoulders.

153

"Ay," said Will, smiling at him in reply; "I can believe that thou art glad to be once again on English soil. France would scarce be to the liking of so direct a soul as thyself."

"Nay; and it was away from her," the Count said, passionately. He spoke lower, yet I caught the words. "Before heaven, Will, my love will consume me, an she still prove cruel; and yet—for thy sake——"

Will made no reply in words; but I can scarce describe the look that answered the Count. In it there was love, and sorrow, and comprehension; yet for whom were the affection, the sadness, the understanding? Ah, for whom?

"And yet," the Count went on, eagerly, pleadingly; "once more, grant me this boon I beg of thee. To me she would never vouchsafe it; yet to thee——"

Will sighed; and as he looked away from the Count his eyes happened to fall upon me, standing still and pale before the entrance to the Globe. He gazed at me an instant, as if the sight suggested an idea. Then he spoke again to the Count.

"Ay, well, I'll grant thee this boon, and the fates favor us. I'll send yon boy as messenger. He's young, and hath a pretty wit, and will please her, methinks.

Remember, no word of this to any of the players else. They know naught positively of my connection with her. They conjecture much, I doubt me not, and some of them visit her, but I have made it understood that I will endure no jesting about the lady."

This, then, was the reason why I had heard nothing of the Countess thus far. Alack, none knew better than I how well Will could keep a secret. None had known of our love-story for a month. This new one of his apparently had been secret for a year.

The Count gave an eager word of assent to Will's last words; but the latter scarce heard him. He had paused suddenly, and was looking dreamily across the Thames. He turned again to the Count.

"Will," he said, "leal comrade, true friend, thou lovest her well; but not as she can be loved. Ah, Will, Will, thou knowest not what love is!"

That passionate speech, that look of tender adoration; both once had been mine; and now—the Count's face was full of despair; and as for me, the world grew dark about me for an instant. The pangs of death were not more sharp than my feelings then. In mine ears there rang as a refrain some old words I had heard once in church:

155

"Love is strong as death; jealousy—jealousy as cruel as the grave!"

"Enough, Will," the Count said at length, after a moment's silence. His voice was low and trembling, and there were tears in his eyes. "I yield thee place; and yet—since she herself is thine, grant me at least this painted image of her that I crave."

They were standing somewhat apart. Will put out his hand and drew the other close.

"Ay, lad," he said, simply, "ay, dear lad. The miniature shall be thine; and perhaps, some day——" He checked himself, and with the Count, walked over to where I stood.

"Cesario," he said—for such was the fanciful name I had chosen for my disguise—"Cesario, I will excuse thee from rehearsal this morning. I have an errand which thou must perform. The boat in which the Count and I came hither still waits below. Cross to the Blackfriars Staircase. There thou wilt find a page clad in crimson awaiting thee. Follow him and thou wilt be taken to the abode of a fair lady. Tell her that thou dost come from Will Shakespeare, and she will give thee a packet for me. See that thou dost lose it not, but bring it hither. Go now, and quickly."

"I like not the sound of the enterprise," I said, not moving. Sooth, I knew not whether I could endure the sight of the Countess that morning. "It hath a woman in it. Therefore, 'tis dangerous."

The Count burst into a laugh; but Will looked at me sternly.

"How now, sirrah!" he said; "'tis not for thee to comment upon the tasks I set thee. Thy part is to obey."

"I am an English lad," I answered, lifting my head defiantly; "and I am no one's slave."

"Nay, but thou art a servant," Will replied, calmly. "Carry not thyself in coxcomb-wise, Cesario. Thy Juliet likes me well, 'tis true; but thou art not the only lad in London. An my errands do not pleasure thee, we'd best part company."

At this threat I succumbed, for it did not suit my plans to leave Will at this juncture of affairs. I grumbled sulkily, and with laggard steps started towards the boat.

"A pettish lad," I heard the Count say, with some amusement, as I went.

"'Tis a new development," Will replied in a puzzled tone. "He hath been gentle and obedient hereto-

fore. Natheless, 'tis but a mood, and 'twill pass, no doubt. He's a good Juliet, and I'll endure him till the play's over, at least."

Most unreasonably hurt by this speech, which was not intended for my ears, I stumbled into the boat, with tears in my eyes; gave a hasty order to the man, and was rowed away from the theatre. As the boat went onward I looked back and saw the Count and Will enter the Globe together, talking busily. As the door closed upon them despair seemed to descend upon me. It was true, then. The dark Countess had bewitched them both. "Ah, Will, Will, thou know'st not what love is!" he had cried; and yet—knew he himself? Passion he had felt, indeed; but love, lasting and true?

"Ah, Will," I cried aloud, not realizing that I did so; "thou know'st not what love is!"

And at that I checked myself, as I saw the boatman looking at me in wondering fashion.

"A pox on thy staring face!" I cried, in sudden passion; "and a murrain on thy snail of a boat. Bring me to Blackfriars within a moment more or I'll prevent the actors of the Globe from hiring thee again. To Blackfriars, fellow, and speedily!"

Chapter XII

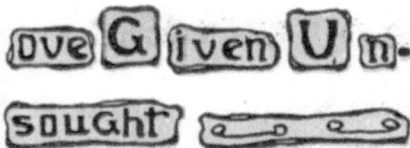

Love Given Unsought

The Countess! By no other name did I ever know her, then, or afterwards, but, sooth, I should have instinctively given her noble title. No coronet was needed upon those lustreless raven tresses, no sceptre in those white, taper fingers to proclaim her right of sway. As I entered the room, in response to the bidding of the lazy, scornful voice that I so well remembered, I saw her, seated by the window on a heap of yellow cushions.

She was dressed in thinnest silk, that clung around her figure, revealing its perfect, glorious curves. Her robe was flame-colored, and as she sat there, blood-red against the light, she seemed to me some baleful spirit incarnate.

I had found the page, as Will had said, and had followed him to a stately house in a fine street. Through many corridors, up many staircases, we had gone together, without speech, and meeting no one, until at last we stood before a certain closed door.

Here the page told me to knock. I obeyed; and in reply the Countess's voice graciously bade me enter.

Now, at last, I stood in her presence.

There was a half-mocking look in her eyes as I came in, but when she saw me she started slightly and sat erect. An attendant was fanning her. With an imperious gesture she bade her cease.

"Whence com'st thou?" she asked, and her dark eyes searched my face, as if she would read it through. They wore an expression that I could not fathom.

"From Will Shakespeare," I answered. My voice was low and trembling; for at sight of her the remembrance of the time when I had last beheld her came over me like a destroying flood.

A smile, scornful, triumphant, just crossed her face, and was gone. So have I seen the evil lightning illumine for an instant the dark and stormy sky. That radiance is not a cheerful nor a holy light.

She threw herself back among the cushions.

"Wherefore?" she drawled, lazily, her eyes still fixed upon my face.

Her indifference angered me. I knew so well what Will's love meant that I burned with sudden rage at her apparent lack of feeling.

"Wherefore?" I repeated, defiantly; and I felt my face flush warmly. "Because—because, in sooth, he loves thee, madam!"

"Doth he so?" she said, smothering a yawn, and she motioned to her woman to begin fanning her again. "The tale is somewhat old, sir page. Hast nothing newer to delight mine ears?"

I gasped with rage.

"An old tale, truly, madam," I answered, fingering my cap with agitated, angry hands; "an old tale, but sweet, to any save a tigress, gloating o'er her prey."

She laughed outright. Her very merriment had a scornful ring. She lifted a fold of her red robe and let it fall again.

"So tigers have crimson coats?" she said, and the lazy amusement in her voice goaded me to the last pitch of exasperation. "Thy knowledge of animals needs addition, little page."

"I know naught of their coats," I answered, immediately, for my hatred of her seemed to spur my wits; "I know naught of their outside seeming; but good sooth, madam, I can discern a tiger's heart."

She looked at me in silence for an instant, and her

163

gloomy, inscrutable eyes seemed to reach my very soul. The laughter was gone out of her face.

"So?" she said at last, suddenly. "Where didst get thy knowledge, boy; thou, a mere child? Art Will Shakespeare's messenger?" She made no pause between her first question and her last; and, indeed, the former words seemed rather to herself than to me.

"Ay, madam," I answered. "I am his messenger; and soothly an easy thing it was for me to reach thee."

"And why, little page?" she said in a softer tone than she had yet used.

"Ah, madam, dost need to ask?" I replied. "Dost not know that love hath wings?"

She leaned forward with sudden, curious eagerness.

"And was it love that brought thee hither?" she said in a low, passionate voice.

"Ay madam," I said, again. "Will Shakespeare's love inspired me, his love brought me hither;" and even as the words passed my lips I realized how bitterly true they were.

She sighed, and sat an instant in deep thought; I remained silent, also, and during that quiet moment a strange and sudden resolution seized me. Why the

singular determination came to me I never knew; but
true it is that then and there I resolved to play my
part; to plead Will's cause as it were my own. I would
show this cruel enchantress what manner of man it
was that she flouted. I would win her for him if I
could. 'Twas all that was left me to do for him. What
was my life, now that he loved me no longer?

"Thou speakest well, little page," the Countess said
at length, rousing from her revery; "so well that it
pleases me to hear thee further. Leave us, Margaret."

The woman cast a glance of surprise, first at her
mistress, then at me; but she did as she was told. Laying down the fan, she bowed to the Countess, and left
the room quickly and silently.

"Ah!" said the Countess, when she was gone, "now
we can talk with more freedom. Come nearer, little
page, and sit by me." She moved over a little and
made an inviting gesture to a place beside her on the
cushions.

"Nay, madam," I said; "not such my place of right,
but here at thy feet. I am love's messenger; and love
is ever humble." I moved forward and knelt beside
her. Sooth, I could not have seated myself where she
indicated, although not for the reason I gave. I feared

165

lest the scorn and loathing I felt for her would over-whelm me in such close proximity.

"So be it, then," said the Countess, with a curious look. Did I dream it or was there truly a strange new softness in her voice? "Thy name?"

"Cesario," I said; "Cesario, and thy servant, madam."

"Cesario!" she repeated; and then again, "Cesario! Cesario!" in a voice that was liquid music. Ah, heavens! what divine melody it was to hear her speak! No wonder that those siren notes drew forth men's hearts to rest with gladness beneath her cruel feet!

"Thou say'st thou art my servant?" she went on, after a moment, and her voice was low and sweet, with no trace in it of mockery nor scorn. "Is't, sooth? Art thou verily my servant, Cesario?"

"Will Shakespeare's servant, madam, and there-fore thine," I replied, perplexed by her tone and man-ner.

"Ah, yes, I had forgot," she said, with a gesture of impatience. "Well, thou com'st from him, thou hast said. Speak on."

"I come on a quest, madam," I replied. "He sent me hither for a packet that thou didst promise him."

166

She looked at me, unheeding, in frowning, thoughtful fashion. "Thou say'st he loves me," she said, suddenly; "ay, so I think; yet—is he worthy of my love?"

"Worthy?" I repeated, angrily; "worthy? Madam, there dwells not the woman on earth who is worthy of him; nay, not even the Queen's Majesty!"

"Thou plead'st well, Cesario," she observed, and I saw her eyes narrow in the curious, cat-like way I remembered well; "thou plead'st well—but I have heard—— Art from the country?"

"Ay, madam," I replied, wondering at what point she aimed.

"Hast known Will Shakespeare long?" she asked, looking at me keenly.

For a moment I was scared most mightily. Should I lie or not? Woman's wits are keen. Was't possible she guessed my sex?

"Ay," I replied, cautiously, at length. "We lived in the same neighborhood."

"Oh, brave!" she exclaimed, with sudden animation. Once more she leaned forward, and fixed her eyes intently upon my face. "Now shall I learn that which I have long desired to know. Hath Will Shakespeare a deserted sweetheart in Stratford town?"

Suddenly, directly, the question was put to me. I stood a moment in a quandary, indeed. Should I tell all, betray him, save myself; or should I choose the nobler part? In a flash my decision was made. I strove to make my voice careless as I answered.

"Nay, 'tis not true. Will Shakespeare hath been always well beloved among both men and maids. His name hath been coupled oft with various lasses' names; especially with one——" I paused, and my voice broke a little; "with whom he once went Maying. I am sure now that he never loved her."

She shot a quick glance at me from under her long lashes.

"Thy voice trembles," she said, abruptly. "Art sorry for her?"

"Ay, madam," I answered, gently; and my traitor voice would tremble still; "ay, for I knew her and I am sure that she loved him, even to the breaking of her heart. Natheless, that was no fault of Will's," I added, hastily.

"Nay; 'tis woman's way," said the Countess, with a tinge of bitterness in her voice. "Cesario, thou lov'st thy master well." She paused a moment; then continued, abruptly. "Dost love no other, boy?"

I stared at her in sudden, horrified comprehension. She rose and came towards me, and for the first time I noticed that we were of a height.

"Cesario," she murmured, again in that tone of low, beguiling music; "Cesario, dost love no other, lad, dear lad?"

Still too dismayed to speak, I stood without moving.

"Cesario," she went on, and I swear her spoken words were sweeter than those that others sing; "Cesario, thou hast plead well thy master's cause. How rarely couldst thou present thine own! Dost love no woman, boy?"

She was close beside me. The perfume of her garments made my senses reel. She swayed her lissome body towards me, and her smouldering eyes sought to draw forth my soul. What good angel gave me voice and words to answer her I know not, but I spoke as by inspiration.

"Ay, I love, I love already, Countess. I love one of my master's favor." She paused at my reply, and the jealous rage that clouded her beauty was horrible to see.

"But how?" she whispered, hoarsely, putting her

169

hand on my arm; "how dost thou love her? Couldst not love more truly—one—like me?"

I made no reply, and she hurried on, eagerly, entreatingly.

"Many men have sought to win my heart, Cesario, but all have I denied. I have sworn never to be conquered, because once, long ago—well, 'tis an old story, and I will not tell it thee. But now—now, I have met my master. Oh, Cesario, have mercy! I love thee."

"The packet, madam?" I repeated, mechanically; and I stayed her as she would have knelt at my feet.

" 'Tis thine," she answered, and she began to unloose a chain from about her neck. " 'Tis thine," she repeated, and she drew forth from her bosom a miniature set with pearls and laid it in my hands. "Remember, 'tis not Will Shakespeare's, but thine. Many have sought the bauble. Behold how freely I give it thee. How wilt thank me?"

"Madam, thus," I answered, bending to kiss the hand that had bestowed the favor, "thus I thank thee, and take my leave, for I have tarried long."

She looked at me and sighed. "As thou wilt," she said at length, submissively, "as thou wilt, so thou dost come again. Thou wilt come?"

"If my master sends," I answered, and as I spoke I moved towards the door, for I longed to leave her.

"He will do so," she said, with a trace of her old mocking manner. "Farewell, then, Cesario, until we meet again." My hand was on the door. With a sudden, sweeping movement she was beside me, and ere I was aware of her intention she kissed me lightly upon the mouth.

"I have kissed thee on the lips," she whispered. "Has woman ever done the like before? Remember, I have sealed thee mine. Farewell, Cesario, my love, my love!"

Blindly, I opened the door and fled along the corridor, down the staircase and thence into the street. How I found my way I never knew; but at length, when I had in some measure recovered my self-possession, I was at the Blackfriars landing. I stood a moment or two striving to collect my thoughts, but, finding the task a vain one, I hailed a boat and started to return to the Globe.

My mind was in a turmoil. Here was a coil, indeed. The Countess was in love with me, or, rather, with my disguise. What should I do? Were it wiser to let the comedy go on, or should I declare myself

and end it forthwith? When I reached the theatre the problem was still unsolved, and with a shrug I dismissed it from my thoughts.

Time must disentangle the situation; 'twas too hard a knot for me to untie.

img_1

omeus and Juliet

Everything was in confusion when I entered the theatre. Rushes were being strewed upon the stage, and the hangings for a tragedy were going up. I saw actors busy here, there, and everywhere; and in the midst of all stood Will, directing, commanding, suggesting. In a dark corner of the stage lolled Sir John, interjecting occasional remarks, which caused the actors to roar with laughter. Count William was nowhere to be seen.

Will saw me at the instant I entered, and hailed me with an air of relief.

"At last, Cesario," he cried; "thou hast tarried long. Come hither, boy, and quickly; for we await thy presence. There's need that we should work briskly; for her Majesty, God save her! has just sent word that she wishes to have this play performed at the palace within a fortnight."

"Thou wilt be in royal company, then, Will," observed Sir John, pretending to wipe his eyes; "thou'lt have no place in thy heart for poor old John."

img_2

"Nay, thou'lt not let him forget thee so long as he hath money in his purse," cried Marlowe, giving the fat man a boisterous slap on the shoulder. Sir John shook under the blow, but he made no attempt to retaliate. He only began to rub the place, with an air of offended dignity. Meanwhile I had come close to Will.

"Hast the miniature?" he said to me in a quick, anxious undertone.

"Ay," I answered, beginning to reach under my doublet for the toy. I had not the least desire to retain it for my own, despite the Countess's words.

"'Tis well, keep it safe," said Will, staying my movement with a quick gesture. "Not here and now. The Count hath gone hence. Moreover, we shall be observed. To-morrow, after the play, will serve."

> "Take, oh, take those lips away,
>   That so sweetly were forsworn;
> And those eyes, the break of day,
>   Lights that do mislead the morn——"

a rich voice began to carol behind us. Will started, and turned with an exclamation of annoyance. I also looked around to see who sang. Behold, 'twas no other

than Sir John, who sat there, his eyes half closed, breathing forth the pathetic words in a voice infinitely rich and sorrowful. One wondered how so rare a thing could be enclosed in so cumbrous a casket.

"Enough!" said Will, imperatively; "no more, Jack. That song belongs not to Romeus and Juliet."

Sir John paused, obediently, but went on humming the air in a kind of undertone. His choice had been accidental, no doubt; but the words he had sung sounded like the voice of fate. Will had been visibly annoyed by them. Was conscience troubling him? I went sorrowfully to my place, the wonder torment-ing me.

The rehearsal began. Master Jonson was Capulet, Marlowe did Tybalt, and Burbadge, Mercutio. The latter took the part of hero, as a rule; but as this was Will's own play, he himself was to act Romeus. How bitter-sweet this last arrangement made the part of Juliet to me! Sometimes it seemed as if I were re-living my own love-story. Had it not also begun in rapture and ended in despair? Again, the contrast between Will's falsehood and the faith of Romeus would cut me to the heart so deep that I found my double part passing difficult to play.

Pale and quiet, I stood on my balcony that afternoon and went through the wooing scene. The miniature lay upon my heart, and seemed to burn my bosom. How careful Will had been that e'en the semblance of the Countess should not be exposed to the players' idle gaze; while I stood here, before them all, for them to jest over and criticise as they would. 'Twas true he knew me not, but had it not been for his falsehood I had not been there at all. That day's long and difficult rehearsal was the final one. The following afternoon occurred the first public performance, in preparation for the great one at the palace. I slept with the miniature under my pillow that night; and methought it gave me uneasy dreams.

The next day I reached the Globe at the appointed time. It was still early, but there was already a great crowd about the theatre. Swearing, singing, jostling one another, they awaited the opening of the doors. The red sign announcing the performance of a tragedy was hung without the building; and as I read it mechanically I thought of how much pleasure it would have given me, in my own person, to witness my husband's triumph. As it was—— I pushed further thought away, and entered.

I found Will pacing up and down the stage. Sir John was at his elbow, following and imitating him, so far as his unwieldy frame would permit.

"Ha, fellow!" cried the latter, importantly, as he saw me. "Why hast tarried so long? Thou'st worried our dear Will."

"I am not subject to your reproof, sirrah!" I answered, tartly, for the speech angered me. Will's brow had cleared as I came in.

"The lad is right, Sir John," he said, somewhat imperiously. "He is here in time and 'tis enough. Thou art not his monitor."

Sir John's tone changed instantly. "Nay, I meant not to be hard on the boy," he said, smiling at me unctuously. "So thou art satisfied, Will, I am, also. Had he not come, remember," he paused impressively, "remember, I offered to take his place."

This remark was made with much gravity, and the speaker's size rendered the idea of his performing Juliet irresistibly ludicrous.

"Thou!" said Will, his face relaxing into a laugh. "Nay, thou shouldst rather play the Nurse. A truce to thy folly, Sir John; and get thee to thy place. Hark! the doors are opening!"

179

We heard the cannon fired without, announcing the opening of the play, and fled to get ready.

A little while later I peeped out between the curtains to get a glance at the audience. There was a full house. The pit was crowded with commoners, who had made up the unruly mob without. The air resounded with their jests and oaths and snatches of song, while they waited for the play to begin. In the balcony beyond sat the gentry; and on each side of the stage were chairs, as yet vacant, which the nobles would occupy later. The last were usually tardy in their arrival, since they felt more secure of their places than did the masses.

Standing in a corner of the pit I saw Robin Greene, looking gloomily about, and, greatly to my surprise, stout Sir John was close beside him. Even as I looked, Robin turned, and the two began to talk together confidentially, with occasional glances towards the stage. So utterly surprised was I that I scarce knew what to do. Surely this amiable converse between Will's sworn enemy and one who accepted his favors and professed to be his friend boded no good to Will himself. For an instant I hesitated as to what course to follow; then the power to decide was taken from me. Will, dressed

in black and wearing a cloak, came forward to speak the prologue, and I left the stage precipitately.

I had already donned my feminine attire, and was struck with a sudden fear lest he should recognize me in these more familiar garments; but he did not. He had seen me only in peasant garb, not in the bravery of Juliet's silks and satins. Moreover, my dyed locks and stained face still stood me in good stead. He looked at me approvingly, and remarked that the gown became me well. Then, as I left the stage, I heard his clear voice begin:

"Two households, both alike in dignity——"

The opening scene followed, amid much applause, and at length it was time for my first appearance. How natural and delightful it seemed to be a maid once more. Now that the time had come, I quite enjoyed my part. Lightly I ran on the stage in answer to the call of Lady Capulet and the Nurse, and cried, blithely:

"Madam, I am here! What is your will?"

As I was in the midst of this scene Count William entered quietly and took his seat at the right of the stage. He caught my eye presently, and gave me a

kindly nod and smile. As for me, I flushed guiltily
for an instant. I could not help wondering what he
and Will would have said had they overheard the conversation between the Countess and myself the day before. As for that kiss at parting——

> "I'll look to like if looking liking move,
>   But no more deep will I endart mine eye
>   Than your consent gives strength to make it fly."

I came back, with a start, to the scene about me
as my own voice uttered the words.

There were sounds of unmistakable approval from
the audience as Juliet's interview with her mother
ended; and the nobles came crowding around Will and
me, congratulating him on his new actor. Will thanked
them for us both, and uttered a few words of com-
mendation on his own account, which were at once
pleasing and distressing to me. These congratulations
ended, the play progressed a little further, and then
came my first trying ordeal, the ball-room scene, where
Romeus and Juliet meet. For some minutes I was on
the stage, scarce knowing what was going on. Then,
ah, then! I was brought back with a sudden rush of
feeling to the play and to my part. Will entered as

Romeus, with Burbadge as Mercutio, and some lesser
actor as Benvolio. An instant later his melodious voice
—who knew so well as I its music and its charm?—
broke across the ordinary accents of the rest:

> "What lady's that, which doth enrich the hand
> Of yonder knight?"

And then came those words which had been spoken
to me, to me alone, one happy May morn—dear God!
how many years ago?

> "Her beauty hangs upon the cheek of night,
> Like a rich jewel in an Ethiop's ear;
> Beauty too rich for use, for earth too dear!"

I swayed an instant where I stood. Gone was the
restless pit, with its noisy, pushing crowd; gone the
roofless theatre, with the blue sky fair above; gone was
the hall of the Capulets and the Italian revellers. Only
Will and I remained; and he stood in a sweet-smelling
country lane on a fair English May Day, while I leaned
from a vine-framed window above; and love undying,
strong as death, entered my poor heart.

Kit Marlowe's fiery Tybalt interrupted my thought
and restored my sense of things present. During the

rapid dialogue that followed, my wits came slowly
back to me. When Will drew near, at last, I was com-
paratively calm; yet when I saw his eyes looking into
mine, with the old, impassioned light; when I heard
his voice, pregnant with love and reverence, I nearly
lost my self-control once more.

> "If I profane with my unworthiest hand
> This holy shrine, the gentle fine is this:
> My lips, two blushing pilgrims, ready stand
> To smooth the rough touch with a tender kiss."

Ah, and if he knew whose lips had last touched
mine! Hurriedly, mechanically, I gave Juliet's reply,
and I fear that all her light speeches were delivered
somewhat heavily. My relief was great when the brief
dialogue ended and I was able to leave Will's side.
Ah, what a lover, what a traitor! cried my heart. Little
wonder he could act passion so well. He had had good
practice; and all my pent-up sorrow and anguish found
vent in the words I cried to the Nurse:

> "Go ask his name. If he be married,
> My grave is like to prove my wedding-bed."

If this scene were difficult, how much more was

Juliet's wooing on the balcony. Alack! could I ever play this part again, with its numberless suggestions of the dear had been? Natheless, once undertaken, it must be gone through with somehow, and so from Juliet's balcony was sighed forth, that day, Anne Hathaway's soul. That scene, which I had helped to make, what sorrow it brought me now! In the old, happy days Will had told me that the first idea of his Juliet was dawning upon him when he met me; and that afterwards he wrote as if inspired. Mine, then, were Juliet's sudden love and heavenly wooing; mine, her hasty marriage; ay, and mine, too, when my task was ended, would be, I hoped, her tragic death. But Romeus would not lie beside her then.

At length the scene ended, leaving me faint and wavering with the effort it had cost me. What mockery were the words that Will's voice sent after me as I staggered from my balcony:

> "Sleep dwell on thine eyes, peace on thy breast!
> Would I were sleep and peace, so sweet to rest."

"Thou art doing well, Cesario," cried Jonson's kindly voice, as I left the stage. He came to me and held out his hand. "If thou dost go on as thou hast

begun, thy fortune's made!" Alack! how little he knew what would make my fortune; a man's smile, a man's love. I tried to thank him, somewhat wearily. Burbadge looked at me compassionately.

"Thou'rt tired, lad," he said. "'Twill be some time before thou wilt appear again, so rest thee. I add my congratulations to Ben's. I shall ask Will to lend thee to me when he finishes the play of which he talks now; a new version of the story of Prince Hamlet. There's a mad, love-lorn girl in it that thou wouldst do well, I know."

"Ay," I answered, laughing somewhat hysterically; "I thank thee, Master Burbadge, thou art right; such a part as that—a mad, love-lorn girl—I love right well to play." And with that I left them, for I felt that if I stayed a moment longer the audience would not wait for Hamlet to see a mad, love-lorn girl rush upon the stage.

The play went on. Mercutio was done with fine effect by Burbadge, and the brilliant, witty part afterwards became a favorite with the London people. Droll Will Kempe made the Nurse utterly humorous, and my scenes with him were a delight, for they relieved the strain to which I was subjected while acting with Will.

At length the wedding in the Friar's cell was celebrated; and then, suddenly, the performance was brought to a standstill. Kit Marlowe had disappeared.

During the alarmed turmoil that followed, while they searched for him, I went once more to the curtains and glanced out at the audience. In the agitations of the play I had forgotten about the singular conjunction of Sir John and Robin Greene in the audience. As I looked out at the pit again, however, I remembered it, and my eye sought them once more. Robin Greene had come close to the stage, and was standing there with an expectant look on his petulant face. Sir John had disappeared.

Scarce had I time to wonder at his absence when my attention was again withdrawn from the audience. Kempe entered, sputtering and angry, bringing with him Marlowe, much the worse for liquor.

"There he sat," he began in a furious tone, so in contrast with his costume as the Nurse that it was very ludicrous; "there he sat, drinking with Jack Falstaff, as if there were no play in progress. Jack was telling his best stories and Kit was pouring wine down his throat, and applauding. Thou renegade! What hast thou to say for thyself?"

But Marlowe had turned sulky and refused to speak. Will, much relieved at sight of him, said a few pacific words, and, after some experiments to see whether Marlowe were sufficiently sober to go through the scene, the play went on.

It had not continued long, however, before Marlowe's sorry plight was discovered by the nobles, and they burst into derisive laughter and satirical gibes, which were taken up in rougher fashion by the pit. This, perhaps, sobered Marlowe, who was accustomed to being a favorite. At any rate, the wavering motion left his legs, and in the ensuing duel with Mercutio he fought magnificently. Finally Burbadge dropped in his supposed death agony, and Marlowe made his exit. A few moments later, in response to Romeus's taunt, he re-entered, and the second duel began.

I was watching from the side, where I could see at once both the scene and the spectators. It seemed to me the mock-duel was lasting longer than it should. Involuntarily, I turned and looked at the audience. Robin Greene was close to the stage now. His neck was craned forward, and upon his face was an expression of eager, delighted malice. I heard murmurs among the nobles. I looked again at the combat on

the stage. The truth came to me with overwhelming conviction. 'Twas no play duel being fought there; and the mimic tragedy was like to prove a real one.

I could not move, I could not cry out. I stood in agony, my eyes fixed upon the flashing swords. An instant later, that which I looked for came. Will fell, with a half-suppressed groan, the blood streaming. Marlowe threw away his rapier and stood in a grandiloquent attitude, a look of drunken triumph on his face. The nobles on the stage arose, horrified. The actors crowded about Will's prostrate figure. The pit, not realizing yet that the play was otherwise than as written, applauded frantically.

As for me, limbs and tongue suddenly seemed loosened. With a scream I ran forward, and, pushing all the rest aside, knelt beside Will, striving to stanch the blood in whose plenteous stream his life seemed flowing forth.

Chapter XIV

 ook **U**pon **T**his **P**icture and **O**n **T**his

At the end of a beautiful summer afternoon, two months later, I sat by the window in Will's lodgings, gazing out at the quiet street beyond. Will lay asleep upon the bed, pale, wasted, yet more like his former self than he had been for many weeks. The room was very still, and my thoughts were busy, as I looked dreamily at the narrow, deserted street and the soaring spire of St. Helen's, visible far above the many roofs. The ordinary, peaceful scene upon which my bodily eyes rested was assuredly in contrast to the tumultuous ones that my spirit's vision beheld.

First I recalled the end of that dreadful duel upon the stage. I remembered how, at length, thanks to Master Burbadge's cool head and wise directions, a doctor had been secured and Will's wound cared for. Then Master Jonson had dismissed the audience, making light of the accident, although his kindly heart was full of anxiety. When he returned to Will's side, how-

ever, he met good news. The doctor had pronounced
the hurt serious, but not mortal, and had said that
with careful nursing he would be himself again within
a few months. Count William at once cried out that
his house should be his friend's shelter; but, much to
my relief, the doctor shook his head. Strange surroundings might aggravate his illness. His own lodgings would be more favorable to his speedy recovery.

So at length it was settled that Will should be re-
moved to his room in the precinct of St. Helen's, and
that I should be his nurse. I was pale and quiet by
this time, not knowing how far I had betrayed my
secret in my first outburst of alarm and agony. In
response to Count William's inquiry whether I would
act as nurse I nodded assent, and forthwith Will was
laid upon a hastily devised stretcher, and several of
the actors took it up, ready to carry to his lodgings.
As they did so, Burbadge glanced around him.

"Marlowe!" he said, as he lifted his share of the
burden, "Marlowe has disappeared."

Count William set his teeth, with an ugly look.

"Ay," he answered; "in the turmoil he hath made
good his escape. I will find him, fear not. There is
a law against duelling. He shall feel its weight."

The Count's words aroused me from my lethargy.

"Find also, then, Robin Greene and Jack Falstaff," I said, speaking in a forced, toneless voice; "find also Robin Greene and Jack Falstaff."

He looked at me in amazement. "Why, lad?" he said, gently. "Why dost thou say so?"

I shook my head and passed my hand across my brow, with a bewildered gesture.

"I cannot tell thee now," I said. "Somehow the words will not come. But do as I beg, prythee, Count William. Find also Robin Greene and Jack Falstaff."

And with that the sentence died upon my lips, as a strange thing happened. The actors had borne their burden carefully and tenderly as far as the entrance to the street. There they set the stretcher down, in order to unbar the door.

The movement, perhaps, caused Will to regain his consciousness. At any rate, he stirred. Noticing this, instantly I rushed to his side, and saw that his eyes were open. They met mine, with a look of entire, delighted recognition. Then, in a weak, far-away voice he breathed my name.

"Nan," he said, softly, tenderly, as if for me alone; and then again, more faintly: "Nan—sweetheart——"

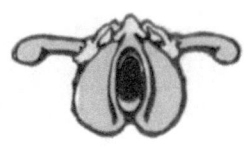

And then he sighed, his eyes closed and he relapsed into unconsciousness once more.

I had much ado to control myself. Methinks I had cared little then had my identity been instantly discovered. Master Burbadge glanced at Master Jonson significantly. I remembered that he knew of my existence, probably of Will's marriage. Count William had not heard the words. Naught was said, however, and without further delay we started on our slow journey to Will's lodgings.

And then, after that terrible afternoon, for two brief months, my love was all mine again. My love! Ay, though faithless to me, he was always and forever my own and only love. The light of my eyes, the glory of my life, was restored to me for a brief space. It was enough. I rejoiced that I had come to London. When he was himself again the Countess would claim him; but now, now—he was mine, all mine.

In his delirium he had never mentioned either my name or hers. His talk was all of the theatre, and plays, and parts. Not once did any Stratford name or place cross his lips. Of Count William and of the various actors he talked freely, although in rambling fashion. He seemed to recognize me as my assumed

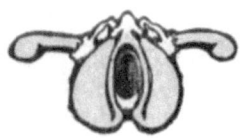

self and called me Cesario. This relieved me much, for I did not choose that he should know me yet. Lately, however, his delirium had ceased, and as he began to gain strength he had said little. To-day, for the first time, he had shown a desire to talk at length, but I had discouraged him, as the doctor bade me.

Naught had been heard of Greene or Falstaff since that day when Will was wounded. When I had grown calmer I had told Count William my reasons for suspecting them, and he had deemed them good. Despite constant searching, however, he had so far been unsuccessful. This was the more remarkable because of Falstaff's unusual appearance. We concluded, at length, that both must have left the city.

Marlowe, with ready and repentant nobility, had come to Count William and given himself up when he had recovered from his drunken brawl and had learned of Will's condition. Count William had promptly caused his imprisonment, and he was still a captive, so far as I knew. I could not help regretting this, for Marlowe had excellent and generous qualities, despite his failings; and in this case I felt that his weaknesses had made him merely the tool of others. As usual, the least guilty suffered, while the really culpable——

I drew my brows together in a little frown of perplexity as I thought this, staring out at the placid sky; and suddenly I was startled by a voice from the bed.

"What's the problem, Cesario? Sooth, there are many in this weary coil of our mortal life." I heard an impatient sigh. "Come hither and talk to me, lad." He smiled teasingly. "Truly, thou must get that ugly frown from thy face, or no sweet woman wilt thou ever play again. Thou lookest now more like Kit Marlowe's Tamburlaine."

I smiled and shook my head as I came obediently and sat beside him.

"Nay," I said, somewhat rashly, "no play of Marlowe's will I ever act in, nor of Robin Greene's, neither——" and then I paused rather abruptly, for I feared my words were imprudent.

He looked at me curiously. "Whence this rage against Kit and Robin—ah, I think I know! Help my memory, Cesario. 'Twas Kit wounded me, was't not?"

He spoke slowly, falteringly, as if tormented by a half-formed recollection. I took quick counsel with myself. Then I decided that uncertainty would be worse for him than to know all. So forthwith I began and told him everything with which my thoughts had

just been busy; of the real duel that had replaced the mock one; of the share that I thought Greene and Falstaff had played in it; and of how Marlowe had given himself up and now lay in prison, by Count William's command.

He started when I said this. "Nay," he said, with energy; "that is ill done of Count William; Marlowe, too, could have eluded justice; instead, he yielded himself up, and should have met with mercy. Well, the remedy will come soon. I will speak with Count William. The London stage needs Marlowe. He——"

Will broke off an instant and lay gazing with bright, unseeing eyes at the blue sky beyond the window, which had now begun to darken into twilight.

"He writes wondrous plays," he continued at length, quietly. "Thou'st been at Paul's, lad, when the organ is pealing forth, and when the music rolls in mighty, majestic waves towards heaven. E'en such is Marlowe's verse—verse that I have not yet equalled, perhaps never shall."

He paused, then continued in a lighter tone: "As for Robin Greene—he is a mere boy, and no doubt is frightened to death now at the result of his plot. He, too, must be spared. But Jack Falstaff——" his tone

199

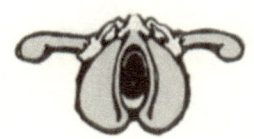

grew stern—"Jack Falstaff is a man, and should have known better. Besides, Robin Greene was my declared enemy; Jack, my pretended friend."

He paused again for a moment; then his brows contracted, as if at some puzzling memory.

"The miniature?" he said, looking at me. "That miniature? Hast it still?"

I started as if stung. He had been speaking of mercy to all who had injured him, and now, for me, whose heart lay beneath his feet, he had naught but cruelty, unconscious yet most bitter. "Ay," I said in a low voice, and turned away my face from him. The afternoon had passed now, and the sky had darkened into night. The outline of the houses was misty.

"Hath she——" he paused an instant—"hath she ever been here?"

"Nay," I said, shortly; then added, unwillingly, "but I have heard Count William say that she hath inquired oft as to thy well-being."

He was silent. I had my head turned from him and could not see his face. At length he sighed. "Well, the miniature," he said. "Let's see it, lad. Little did I deem, when I sent thee for it, that 'twould be so long before mine eyes beheld it."

Obediently I drew it forth from the place in my bosom where it had rested many weeks. Little had I thought, either, that its hated presence would be near me for so long. It was still upon the chain which had held it when she gave it me. I freed it from my neck and laid the porcelain trifle in his hand.

"A light," he said. "Bring hither a candle, Cesario."

I obeyed. He lifted the miniature feebly and held it so that he could gaze at it. Thus he lay long, but at last he broke silence.

"A fair face, Cesario," he said; "a fair face. Is't the mirror of as fair a soul?"

He spoke as if to himself rather than to me, but I answered.

"I know not," I said; then added, desperately, "Count William deems it so."

A spasm of pain crossed his face.

"Ay, I know," he answered, gently, and again gazed reflectively at the painted bit of porcelain. The eyes, insolent, yet dreamy, looked back at him. The lustreless raven hair lay heavy over the white brow. The countenance was mocking, elusive, as in life——

"A fair face," he said again, musingly. "Methinks I have never seen a fairer."

I blew out the candle with a quick breath and answered his words on impulse. Why I spoke as I did I know not. Methinks the pent-up jealousy and anguish of months suddenly burst the bounds so sternly set before them.

"Thou didst deem otherwise once," I said, and gazed out into the night with tragic eyes. The world was dark now, ah, very dark! Even so, the sun of my life had set, and soon the night of death and darkness would encompass me. The river—the river lay near, flowing—flowing swiftly to the sea. It bore many things upon its bosom. What if I entrusted to its kindly care a broken heart, a weary body——

Will started at my words. I could feel his eyes upon me.

"What mean'st thou?" he said, imperiously. "What mean'st thou?"

I did not turn from the window. "The face of the Countess is fair, indeed," I said; "dusky as night is her hair—as a night without stars. Her eyes—fathomless wells of truth?—of falsehood?—who shall read them? Ay, she is fair; but once thou didst find charm, master, in a different face."

I heard the quick turn of his body in the bed be-

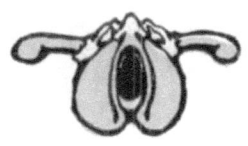

hind me, his fast, irregular breathing; but he did not speak.

" 'Twas a face," I went on, "a face sorrowful, yet fair; at least, so thou didst call it once. Her eyes were very dark—and sad, until thou didst come into her life. Then they grew joyous for a while. I wonder if they be sad now. Her hair was golden——"

He interrupted me with a sharp cry. "Where didst thou learn all this?" he queried.

I went on, unheeding the appeal in his voice.

"Men say she went mad for love—poor fool! 'Tis woman's way. What matter? Thou hast the Countess now."

Again he cried out, in a way that startled me— imperious, bewildered:

"How knowest thou this; how knowest thou?"

But I was looking out into the night, and I did not turn.

" 'Will he not come again? Will he not come again?'

"Thus she sang," I said. " 'Tis passing sad, her story. I had it from a Stratford lad."

I turned now and looked at him. The room was too dark for us to see each other, but I felt his eyes

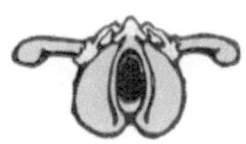

striving to search my face. He had risen into a half-sitting position. He sank back now with a deep, long-drawn sigh.

"Thou know'st my story in some strange way," he said in a low, trembling voice. "Has she written in these months?"

"Nay," I answered, truthfully.

"Can aught be wrong?" he murmured. "Thou know'st Stratford, then, lad. Light the candles and tell me more."

As I obeyed the first part of his command, wondering how I could evade the second, a shadow fell across the threshold.

"Well, prince of poets," exclaimed a rich, lazy voice that we both knew well, "how goes the world with thee?"

She swept a magnificent curtsey, and came forward into the light.

It was the Countess, fair and stately, her crimson robes sweeping the floor, her velvet cloak half falling from her shoulders. For an instant she stood thus; then Will spoke in a voice curiously suppressed.

"Be seated, Countess," he said. "Cesario, fetch hither a chair." He paused an instant as I obeyed

204

him, glancing from the Countess's face to mine with evident indecision. Then, in a curiously apologetic tone, he continued:

"St. Helen's is near. Go thither, Cesario, and wait upon the church steps until I send for thee."

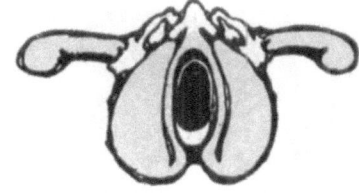

Chapter XV

**Y** the **C** **hurch**?

Furiously, blindly, I stumbled down the stairs and out into the night. So insensible was I to all things except the inward fire of my jealous rage that I saw and heard naught until I had been seated for some time on the broad steps of St. Helen's.

The corner I had chosen was mercifully obscure, and there, crouched upon the unyielding stone, I wept and ground my teeth and clenched my fists in impotent, overwhelming despair. There, in the well-lit room she, the beautiful sorceress, sat with him, while here in the darkness I lay, alone. Who and what was she, this shameless, gorgeous woman, who, despite her noble title, her costly attire, came at nightfall, unattended, to a man's lodgings? Why had she come? Wherefore had I been sent away? A flood of conjectures and uncertainties overwhelmed my brain.

It was very dark on the church steps, and St. Helen's was a quiet district. I was weary and unstrung in mind and body. Beyond a certain point of endurance even extreme anguish cannot go. At length

nerves and brain alike relaxed. My hard vigil was ended and I slept.

How long I thus forgot my troubles I know not. I awoke suddenly, with a start. The church was light now, and within I heard the choir practising. Fragments of an anthem floated out, interrupted by numerous silences, during which, no doubt, the choirmaster was explaining and instructing. I lay still an instant, listening dully. They were chanting the "Magnificat."

"He hath showed strength with His arm: He hath scattered the proud in the imagination of their hearts."

Thrice were the words repeated, each time with some slight change in rendering, due, probably, to the choirmaster's suggestion. The third time I noticed languidly that one of the church doors had been left open, and that the brightness from within streamed past the corner where I crouched, out into the street itself. My eyes followed the shaft of light and I sprang upright with a cry. In its full radiance stood the Countess, looking at me. Her crimson draperies seemed, in my excited imagination, to radiate flames.

When she saw me looking at her, in scorn and abhorrence, she held out her hands beseechingly.

"Cesario! Thou cruel one!" she barely breathed in a tone of tenderest reproach. "Where hast thou been all these long, long weeks?"

I raised my hands to shut out the sight of her despicable beauty, her devilish charm.

"Thou hast two victims already, madam," I said, and I took no pains to hide my disgust and hatred. "Thou shalt not have a third. I return to my master," and I moved a step to pass her. She spread out her arms to bar my way. I could not go without creating an outcry. I paused. She seized my hand in both of hers, and I felt her burning lips upon it.

"Ah, Cesario," she whispered, "how beautiful are even contempt and anger on thy lips! Nor all my wit nor reason can hide my passion for thee. Cesario, be not cruel. Men have deemed me beautiful. Canst not love me a little, even a little, Cesario? Many have sued me; behold, I lay my heart at thy feet; it is thine! Wilt thou spurn it?"

The choir in the church had been silent for a space. Now they burst forth into the next strain of the "Magnificat."

"He hath put down the mighty from their seat, and hath exalted the humble and meek."

Methinks I was half mad with rage and despair, or else the devil himself tempted me in the Countess's guise. At any rate, a fiendish plan entered my mind that instant; a cruel scheme, since it involved the happiness of three others and would make my lot no better. Yet my idea seemed sweet to me then because it spelled revenge.

The holy words pealed forth again, joyously:

"He hath put down the mighty from their seat, and hath exalted the humble and meek."

I looked at the Countess, bending her proud head before me, and a triumphant smile touched my lips. Now I shudder to think how I applied the meaning of those sacred words, first spoken for so holy a reason; but then they seemed sent from heaven to suggest to me my vengeance.

The Countess looked up and saw my smile. Her face lighted with joy, and she drew closer to me.

"Thou wilt love me, Cesario? Thou wilt——" she hesitated an instant. "Wilt thou even—wed me?"

"Listen, madam," I said, and I put my arm around her, repugnant as the touch of her sinuous body was to me. She gave a cry of joy at my embrace, and clung

to me. "Beseech thee, think a moment. Thou knowest me not. Remember, I warn thee. Thou knowest me not."

Some last fragment of compunction made me give her this hint. She was too blinded by her infatuation, however, to heed my words.

"It matters not," she murmured, and she laid her dusky head upon my shoulder. "It matters not who thou art. I love thee."

"Enough, then, madam," I responded. I stood, holding her in my arms, my eyes staring straight forward in cold, unseeing fashion as I elaborated my plan. "Enough! I make thee, then, this promise. At Michaelmas I will go to church with thee."

She gave a little cry, half delight, half disappointment.

"So long to wait! Ah, Cesario! Why not to-morrow?"

"Because, madam," I answered, steadily, "neither Count William nor my master must know aught of this until after—after I have been at church with thee." I held carefully to the phrase I had chosen. "At Michaelmas it is rumored that her Gracious Majesty will request a performance of Romeus and Juliet at the palace.

If that prove true, I am bound to act Juliet, and I cannot—go to church with thee—until that, day."

"But why," she whispered, "why not wed me tomorrow, and let the marriage remain a secret until Michaelmas?"

"Because, madam," I said, again, "because, after I have been at church with thee, methinks I shall not act Juliet nor any other part again."

She looked at me in deep thought, her eyes narrowing. For an instant she seemed again the haughty, wary creature I had seen beneath the willows at Stratford. Then her face relaxed, and she smiled and sighed together. No wonder she could play with men's hearts.

"Be it so," she whispered low, in that voice which was liquid music. She laid her head upon my shoulder once again. "Cesario, Cesario, must I do all the wooing? Give me my betrothal kiss."

I bent my lips and touched hers calmly.

"Until Michaelmas, then, adieu, Countess," I said.

She drew herself erect instantly.

"Until Michaelmas," she repeated. "Shall I not see thee until then? Oh, Cesario, be not cruel!"

"No, madam," I answered, firmly, for on this point I was determined to have my way; else the rest of my

plans might miscarry. "Bethink thee and thou wilt see that I am wise. Should we be meeting constantly, suspicion assuredly would be aroused. We desire no hint of our undertaking to escape—until Michaelmas."

She bent her beautiful head and stood a moment in troubled silence, biting her red lips and clenching her hands. At length she roused herself with a sigh.

"Thou art right," she said. "Thou art right, Cesario. Farewell, then, until we meet again on the morning of Michaelmas. Let our wedding take place at Paul's. 'Tis a church I love well."

I agreed, for it mattered little what place she chose for a marriage that would never take place. Again she offered me her lips.

"Until Michaelmas, adieu," she murmured, as I once more kissed her. Then she went down the church steps, her crimson gown brilliant in the light that streamed from the still open door. The choir had finished the "Magnificat" long since, but now they were going over bits that the exacting master had found unsatisfactory.

As the Countess, brilliant as an evil spirit, lithe as a panther, passed from my view, these words floated after her:

"He hath filled the hungry with good things, and the rich
He hath sent empty away."

I fell upon my knees in a sudden revulsion of feeling. There, yonder, she went, the rich woman, and how empty was the prospect towards which she looked with joy so delirious! And I—I, kneeling here upon the church steps—ah, how good was the revenge which satisfied the hunger of my hatred!

Chapter XVI

Take, oh Take Those Lips Away . . . .

I found Will asleep when I returned that night, and the next morning he did not mention the Countess, nor did I. In a few days we were both busy with thoughts of the coming performance at the palace. The command had, indeed, been sent by her Majesty that our company should play Romeus and Juliet before her; and Will was like a boy in his delight. Master Jonson and Master Burbadge shared his pleasure with unselfish joy, and, indeed, all the company seemed glad that their comrade had such an honor bestowed upon him. The only drawback was Will's bodily condition; but that improved steadily from the time the Queen's command arrived, and the doctor gave it as his opinion that Will would be fully able to play by Michaelmas. So, as soon as possible, he and I were once more rehearsing our old familiar parts as lovers.

The first time Will left his room, he went with

Count William to the prison and ordered Marlowe's release. What was said at that time I never knew; but thenceforth Marlowe treated Will with a dog-like fidelity and devotion touching to see, and singular in one of his haughty carriage and careless manners. Robin Greene and Jack Falstaff had not yet been heard of. They seemed to have buried themselves in the earth.

During those weeks I never saw the Countess. She was faithful to our compact; and Will did not speak of her. I wondered a little at this, but finally concluded that the excitements of the preparation for the palace had driven her temporarily from his mind. To me she seemed like a nightmare; one that had tormented me in the past, that would come again, but which now was not. I tried to forget her until Michaelmas.

The miniature had disappeared. I never saw it on Will's person, and I thought he must have it hidden among some secret treasures. I tormented myself for awhile with conjectures about this, but finally dismissed them with a shrug. At Michaelmas, if my plan prospered, all would become clear.

And at length September, cool and beautiful, came, passed, was nearly ended. The Feast of St. Michael

and All Angels dawned, and with it the thought of my revenge.

As I finished dressing that morning I saw, slipped under my door, a small, flat package secured by a crimson ribbon. Inside was a lock of lustreless raven hair tied with a blood-colored love knot. 'Twas at once a token and a reminder, as I knew well. Had there been a fire at hand I would have burned the accursed thing. I dared not leave it lying in my room. I thrust it into my bosom, with loathing.

We were to be at the theatre at noon. The day before I had begged Count William and Will to meet me at the entrance to Paul's at ten. They had marvelled at my request, and Will had demurred slightly, since it would be a busy morning for him. At length, however, when I said the matter was urgent, they consented, and so everything pointed to a successful consummation of my plans.

I broke my fast but frugally that morning. I was filled with alternate dread and triumph. Soon, soon would come the hour for my revenge. Then—Marlowe indeed had stabbed Will's body; but I would kill his heart. Alack, alack! in what a coil was I involved. Natheless, I could not bear my anguish longer! I

could not! And, starting up with the thought, I threw down a coin to pay for the food I had eaten, and rushed away to fulfill my appointment.

It was just ten as I neared Paul's, and, prompt as I was, the Countess had reached there before me. I noted, with relief, that neither Count William nor Will was with her. I did not desire that they should come too soon.

When she saw me, she stretched out her hands to me, regardless of the numerous passers-by. Paul's is a busy place, and its nave is a fashionable promenade. We were quite near the entrance.

"Cesario," she cried in a joyous undertone; "at last, at last! Didst receive my token? Is all arranged?"

"Ay, madam," I said, truthfully, although I had engaged no priest, which was what she meant; "ay, madam, but we must wait a little. I have invited two friends—as witnesses——" I turned to look for them, and the words I had been about to speak remained unuttered. I saw Will and the Count approaching. Her gaze followed mine. She caught her breath inward with a sharp sound, and looked at me piercingly, piteously. For a moment I was sorry for her.

There was an instant's silence. "What means this?" she said at length, in a quick, incisive whisper. "What means this?"

"It means, madam," I answered, "that the comedy is near its close."

I caught her hand and held it, despite her wild effort to withdraw it.

"Let me go," she cried, although still in a low tone. "Art mad, Cesario?"

"No, madam," I said, and I caught her other hand, thus making her my prisoner; "I am not mad now, although I have been, and may be. Natheless, I hope my remedy is near."

And thus we stood until the Count and Will reached us.

"What unwilling fair one hast thou there, Cesario?" called Will, his face alight with mischief. The Countess had averted her face and he did not recognize her at once. Count William opened his lips to fling a gay gibe at me, but closed them with the jest unuttered. Will gave a sharp exclamation. The Countess had raised her head and looked at them.

For a moment no one spoke. Then Will turned to me.

"Explain," he said, and his voice was cold with contempt. "Thou brought'st us hither, sir. Explain!"

I had been trembling; but at his challenge I grew suddenly calm and collected. My all was placed upon this throw.

"Surely, no explanation is needed," I said. "The Countess——" I indicated her by a slight gesture— "the Countess has done me the honor of promising to be my bride. I have summoned you as witnesses."

Count William was very white. He uttered a fierce oath at my words and started towards me. Will's hand restrained him.

"Peace, friend," he said, gently, "we are in a crowd. Make no demonstration here." Then to me, once more coldly, "When was all this arranged?"

"A month ago," I answered, airily, "a month ago we agreed to go to church to-day," and I drew out from my bosom the raven lock of hair tied with the crimson love-knot.

"Let me go," said the Count, fiercely, struggling beneath Will's restraining hand and turning blazing eyes on me as he saw the trifle in my hand. "Let me choke the lie in his throat, the accursed, soft-spoken traitor!"

"Nay," cried the Countess, wrenching herself free from me and standing erect. "Nay, thou shalt not blame him. I loved him at first sight. I made him woo me. Thou shalt not punish him, thou shalt not!"

There was something noble in her supreme self-surrender. Again I felt a pang of pity for her. Will glanced around him at the gathering crowd. It struck me for the first time that he was curiously calm.

"Let us go to a more retired place," he said to the Count.

"No," replied the latter, furiously. "I will punish him here and now for his insolence and treachery."

I put my arm around the Countess.

"You refuse to act as witnesses, then?" I said, and smiled at her tenderly. At the look, the caress, Count William's self-control gave way. He flung off Will's hand as if it were a feather and whipped out his rapier.

"Thy sword," he gasped. "Thy sword, fellow! Ah, thou hast none!—Thine, friend, prythee," courteously, to one of the bystanders. It was proffered him instantly. He drew it out of its sheath with a lightning flash of steel and struck the Countess's love-token from out my hand. "Here, thou low-born milk-sop!" he cried, tendering the borrowed weapon to me.

"I will soil my hands by killing thee, and so leave in the world one whining Judas less."

I turned white. Here was a development of which I had not dreamed. I had a true woman's horror of swords, and knew naught about fencing. Sooth, I would die bravely, gladly, but not in this fashion. I looked about me desperately for means of escape.

The Count saw my shudder and my pallor, and laughed derisively.

"A brave lover!" he said. "The mere look of a sword makes him chalk-white. See how he dangles it in his hand. What! must I kill thee without the pretense of a duel? So be it, then!" He lifted his rapier.

"End it quickly, Count. The crowd grows," said Will, glancing about him.

The Countess uttered a piercing scream and held out her hands beseechingly to the crowd that now hemmed us in, calling for help. The sympathy of the people was against us, however, for the cause of the quarrel had been whispered from one to another.

"Not even thy tears shall save him, Countess," cried Count William, furiously. "Come, fellow, lift thy point. Thou hast played with two hearts, madam; 'tis fitting that thine own should break."

I lifted the weapon I held in gingerly fashion, and the crowd roared with laughter. The Countess sobbed. Will looked at me with a smile of contempt. A mist rose before my eyes.

The Count lunged at me furiously. His point barely missed my heart. With the narrow escape such courage as I had suddenly deserted me. I forgot my disguise, remembered nothing save the present. I was all woman again. I began to sob, and, dropping the sword, ran forward and fell at Will's feet, embracing his knees in an agony of terror.

"O Will," I cried, "Will, save me! O Will, be not so cruel to me!"

There was another great burst of laughter from the crowd, echoed derisively by the Count. But Will did not share in their mirth. He looked down at me, amazement and contempt struggling for the mastery in his expression. Then suddenly his countenance changed. He bent towards me and gazed searchingly into my eyes. Then recognition flashed into his face. He lifted me suddenly, drew me to his heart and laid my tear-stained countenance upon his breast.

"Nan," he whispered in my ear, "Nan, dear Nan, my sweetheart and my wife!"

Chapter XVII

 An instant thus we stood. Then Count William's voice broke the spell that bound us.

"What means this?" he said. "Thy kindliness of heart, Will, hath made thee strangely forgetful of friendship's ties. Release the lad and let me conclude his punishment."

"The watch!" cried a boy's shrill voice suddenly on the outskirts of the crowd. "The watch approaches."

The Count stood his ground; not so the idle rabble that surrounded us. They gave cries of alarm in various keys, and melted away like dew before the sun. The man who had lent the sword to me left it where it lay, and fled. Count William sheathed his, and folded his arms. When at length the officers of the law did approach, puffy and important, he bestowed a gold-piece or two upon them, which instantly rendered them blind and obsequious. At their departure he turned to me again.

I had raised my head, but still stood with Will's

arm encircling me in protecting fashion. The Countess had sunk down on the church steps, and sat there pale and erect, awaiting the outcome of the scene.

"Now 'tis quiet enough in all conscience, and the watch will not trouble us again. Pick up thy sword, Cesario."

"Nay," interposed Will, releasing me, and himself taking up the weapon. "Nay, Will, if thou'rt bent on fighting, thou must e'en fight me."

The Count stared at him in utter amazement. The Countess rose from where she sat and came forward.

"And why?" the former demanded at last, recovering his voice.

Will put his arm around me again. "Because," he answered, "because—I know not how nor why, but a miracle hath been wrought. An instant since, Cesario, my page, stood here. Now 'tis Anne Shakespeare, my dear and honored wife."

I gave a cry and again hid my glowing face upon his shoulder.

The Count was silent from sheer amazement, but I felt his eyes upon me. The Countess gave a curious cry, whether of pain, of surprise, of disappointment, it

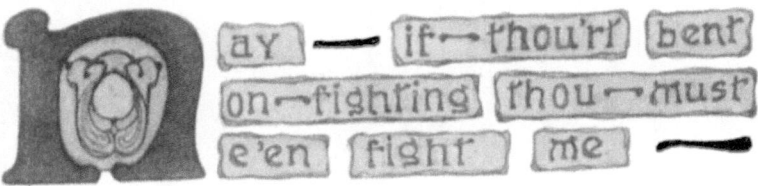

NAY — if thou'rt bent
on fighting thou must
e'en fight me —

would be difficult to say. I raised my head again and looked at her. She was staring at me, her eyes large, her face pale.

"A woman!" she muttered, as if to herself. "A woman!"

Then she paused, and her expression became inscrutable and mocking as of old. She gave a hard little laugh.

"I have been the heroine of a pretty comedy, it seems," she said, her eyes still full upon me and her face ablaze with anger. Then suddenly her expression softened and grew curiously wistful.

" 'Tis a Paradise I cannot share," she said, slowly; and she meant our love, methinks. "I might have known it. Only the innocent can enter those white gates. I dreamed that I might—but I was wrong. The truest love of my poor sinful soul has been given to a shadow."

She came towards us, and gave her hand to Will to kiss. He bent over it obediently. Then suddenly she leaned forward, and once again, for the last time, her lips touched mine.

"Farewell, my shadow love," she said, smiling sombrely, "and farewell, Mistress Shakespeare. Love

233

and loyalty are not altogether dreams, though I have sometimes thought them so. Your secret is safe—Cesario!"

Her face was convulsed with grief for an instant as she looked at me. It was as if she gazed on the corpse of one beloved. And so, indeed, she did. Then, composing herself, she bowed slightly to each of us and went down the street alone. We stood watching her until the last glimmer of her scarlet robe had disappeared. Then Count William broke into a cry.

"Ah, Will, I love her, love her still! What shall I do to make her mine?"

Will shook his head and laid his hand, with a caressing gesture, upon the Count's shoulder.

"Patience, Will, patience! She is broken now over the shattering of her dream; but that she could love even a shadow so sincerely shows that her heart is noble, as I have deemed it ever. Surely, thy long devotion will touch her at last. Wait and love——"

"As thy lady here hath done," said the Count, courteously interrupting. He knelt before me. "Mistress Shakespeare, I know not how nor why thou wearest this disguise, but thy secret is safe with me also. I hope thou wilt forgive my hasty rudeness a

234

while since. Prythee remember I labored under a mistake."

I gave him my hand, and smiled in token of forgiveness. He pressed his lips upon it and then rose.

"Farewell, Will," he said, drawing his cloak about him, "farewell until noon—— Ah, where now will be thy performance at the palace?"

Will's face fell, and he looked at me in comical perplexity.

"Nay," I said, readily, although I blushed; "why need any change be made? None knows who I am save you two and the Countess, and none need be told. Let the play go on."

Will shook his head doubtfully, but his face cleared in spite of himself.

"The lady is wise," said Count William. "Let it be as she says, Will. Thou canst get no other Juliet at this late hour, and the change would create comment."

"So be it, then," said Will. " Thou'st played thy part so well, Nan, that 'twill do no harm to play it a little longer. Then to Stratford, and an end to mysteries."

Again applauding his decision, Count William

235

bowed and left us. We watched him, also, out of sight, his golden hair and gleaming blue satin shining in the sun. Then Will turned to me.

"Sweetheart," he said, and his tone was as love-filled as of old; "sweetheart, what means it all? I am bewildered. Prythee enlighten my darkness."

We began to walk down the street together.

"It grows near noon," I answered, "and we shall not have time for many words now; but ere I enlighten thy darkness thou must let the sun rise on mine."

And then, as we went slowly towards the boat landing, I told him all that had happened in those dreary months since we parted. I began with the conversation I had overheard beside the willows. Then followed the story of my madness, at which he groaned, and murmured words of love and commiseration. Finally I narrated how and why I had come to London. Then I paused an instant and looked at him.

"Will," I said, and my voice trembled, betraying the anguish that had tormented me so long, "thou seem'st thy old, dear self to me, and yet—didst thou—didst thou ever love her?"

He looked at me with so amazed an expression that my question was answered before he spoke.

"Never," he said, and his voice was as wondering as his face; then, in a pained way, "Nan, hadst no faith in my truth and honor?"

"Forgive me," I murmured, with instant repentance; "forgive me; and yet——"

"Yet—perhaps thou wert justified. She thought, too, that I loved her for a while," he went on, half to himself. "So did Count William at one time.

"A woman's face, with nature's own hand painted,
    Hast thou, the master mistress of my passions;
A woman's gentle heart, but not acquainted
    With shifting change, as is false woman's fashion.
An eye more bright than theirs, less false in rolling,
    Gilding the object whereupon it gazeth;
A man in hue, all hues in his controlling,
    Which steals men's eyes, and women's souls amazeth."

He paused and turned to me, his face illumined. " 'Twas of Count William I wrote thus, Nan," he said. "Is't not true? Hath he not a woman's face in beauty, and a woman's gentle heart? Ah, loyal, loving friend! Deem not, however, dearest, that I thought of thee when I spoke of false women. Nay, 'tis the majority I mean; and Nan—Nan, thou hast been a lad in London long enough to know that of most women it is sooth."

237

"But the Countess—what of her?" I said, with diffidence.

"The Countess? Ah!" he said, with the same strange, speculative look he had worn before when speaking of her.

"How sweet and lovely dost thou make the shame
　　Which, like a canker in a favorite rose,
　Doth spot the beauty of thy budding name.
　　O, in what sweets dost thou thy sins enclose!"

He paused again, and looked at me with a curious expression.

"Dost understand?" he said.

I did as in a lightning flash. Many things I had not comprehended were now made clear. I remembered the Countess's singular freedom of dress and manner; and how she had come alone, at nightfall, to Will's lodgings. I recalled the tragic despair with which she had spoken of her "poor sinful soul" a short space since. Not of ordinary human frailty are such tones used. I looked at Will in sudden, wide-eyed comprehension.

"Yet," I began, doubtfully, "she lives in a right stately house—she's called the Countess——"

"And 'tis no nickname," interrupted Will, "and 'tis in the halls of her ancestors that she dwells. Sorrow and anguish she hath brought to her proud house, and yet—and yet—despite all, she hath a noble heart. She gave it freely to thee in thy disguise, and some day, perhaps, Count William——"

He fell into a thoughtful silence, looking into space with the calm, large gaze that saw broader and deeper than other men. But I could not forbear interrupting his revery. Although my doubts as to his loyalty were laid at rest, my curiosity was not yet satisfied.

"But Will," I said, "Will, thou didst long so for her miniature; thou didst bid me keep it safely;—oh, and she deemed that thou didst love her—and Count William, that day by the Globe, when thou first didst send me to her——"

He laughed, and patted me lightly on the cheek.

"What, sweeting, still wondering? Listen, then, and learn all the heart of thy true lover in a few words as brief as may be. Count William was kind to me when I first came to London. Among other things, as our friendship grew, he confided to me his passion for the Countess. I visited her with him. For a time

239

I think her fancy was taken by me, and so thought Count William. While he labored under this delusion he was nobly willing to leave the field to me. He begged, however, that he might have the miniature which she had lightly offered to me as a keepsake one day. 'Twas this conversation thou didst overhear between us. After thou hadst left us, then I told him, in confidence, of my marriage, and my undying love for thee. Since that day he has known that my heart was never hers, nor ever would be. That night, when she came to my lodgings, 'twas to seek thee, as I know now. Then I could not understand her appearance, but seized the opportunity to plead Count William's cause. I did not know then why my words were so unavailing. 'Twas because Cesario filled her heart and mind. And now—poor, noble, misguided soul—what will be the end?"

Again he sank into thought, but again I was not quite satisfied.

"But Will," I said, timidly, "thou didst visit her—thou didst write poetry about her—Count William and she both thought——"

He turned to me with a swift, indignant gesture.

"Nan," he said in a tone of quiet reproach, "Nan,

have I deserved this? Nay——" as I instantly craved his pardon—"let us make an end, for our comrades wait, and in a few minutes more thou must be Cesario again, and Romeus and Juliet must fill all our thoughts. Ever in body and soul have I been loyal to thee, Nan. Never hath a day passed since our parting that thy image hath not been in my heart, and thy long, mysterious silence has caused me bitter grief. Yet, for thy own sake, I could not leave London. Thou hast seen how I am bound by the theatre, and lately by my illness. As for the Countess—my name has, indeed, been coupled with hers, for I frequently accompanied Count William on his visits to her. Never hath it been so associated with just reason, though, I swear. I have sought to further his cause. The poetry I have just now said to thee was written for that purpose. All the interviews, few in number, I have ever had with the Countess alone have been towards the same end. There is another reason—ay, I freely admit it."

His face lit with mysterious fire, as I had seen it oft at Stratford when he told me of his dreams.

"That reason I may tell to thee alone, Nan," he went on, slowly. "None other would understand. I am a poet, Nan. All nature is the book I read, and

all mankind. Naught is too high, naught too low for me to find of interest and of value. Each man and woman, every tree and flower, all words and gestures that I see and hear are preserved in the world that lives within my heart and soul. There are many figures in it, Nan, and many scenes. Some of our Stratford walks and talks dwell there, and London haunts of vice and sorrow. Our love story and Count William's are constantly re-lived in that world within. Jack Falstaff, humorist and traitor, exists in my dream universe, and the Countess, mocking and inscrutable; and I think of all these, and many others; and live with them, and strive to enter into their minds and souls; and then——"

His tone, which had been exalted and mysterious, broke off with a little laugh. He ended in matter-of-fact fashion.

"And some day, I hope, in one way or another, this dream-world shall materialize into comforts for thee and the babe, sweetheart; and that Will Shakespeare shall become a respectable Stratford citizen."

I leaned against him in perfect content. We had reached the boat-landing now, and the little craft he had signalled to take us to the theatre was coming rapidly towards us.

"And so," he ended, "the Countess is not the one woman in the world for me, as thou art, beloved, but she is one of many, whom it is alike my pleasure and my business to study and to admire. Art satisfied now, sweetheart, sweetheart? Ah, I love thee better for thy jealousy. Thou wert less a woman without it; but it was groundless, dear. Listen; among the poems I have written for Count William and his wooing, now and again I have slipped interludes, which are for thee and me. Canst guess of whom this speaks?"

The river lay fair and sparkling in the noon sunlight. I stood gazing at it dreamily, recalling how, a few hours since, I had thought to seek its waters to still the anguish of my heart forever. Ah! what a contrast was the happy present, while the voice dearest to me in all the world murmured in my ear the last conclusive witness of his loyalty and love:

"From you I have been absent in the spring,
    When proud-pied April, dressed in all his trim,
Hath put a spirit of youth in everything,
    That heavy Saturn laughed and leaped with him.
Yet nor the lays of birds, nor the sweet smell
    Of different flowers in odor and in hue,
Could make me any summer's story tell,

Or from their proud lap pluck them where they grew.
Nor did I wonder at the lilies white,
  Nor praise the deep vermilion in the rose;
They were but sweet, but figures of delight,
  Drawn after you, you pattern of all those.
Yet seemed it winter still, and you away;
  As with your shadow, I with these did play."

Chapter XVIII

 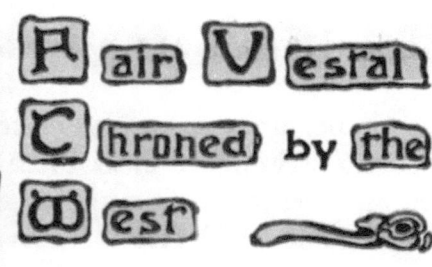

A air Vestal Chroned by the West

We were late at the theatre, and with a laughing jest regarding our delinquency we jumped from the boat and rushed rapidly up the path to the doorway. The outside of the Globe was deserted, but as we reached the entrance we heard angry voices wrangling within. Two of them struck upon my ear with strange familiarity. As we entered, both of us stopped short and I gave an exclamation of surprise.

There before our eyes stood the couple who had disappeared so entirely from the face of the earth during the last few months—Robin Greene and Jack Falstaff.

The former, always slender, was emaciated now, and his petulant young face was drawn and haggard. Methought it wore, also, a certain look of shame. Jack Falstaff, however, was as mountainous and self-possessed, as urbane and calm, as ever.

247

The other actors were crowded around them, excitedly striving to eject them from the theatre. With Robin Greene this was possible; but Jack Falstaff's bulk made his forcible removal a giant's task. Moreover, the gentle reproaches, the calm self-assurance with which he met their threats and protests, made them laugh as of old, despite themselves.

"Ah, here is my dear friend Will!" cried the stout sinner as he saw us. "Now all will be well with us. Congratulations, Will. I heard that thou wert to have thy play performed at the palace, and I, being of noble birth by rights, as thou knowest, came to assist thee. Robin and I have been wandering in France and have just returned." He gazed, smiling and complacent, full into Will's face, but he met there no response. Those hazel eyes, always so ready to twinkle at his folly, were calm with quiet scorn. The countenance, usually so mobile, was coldly expressionless. The actors surrounding us fell into a strained silence, awaiting an unexpected development.

For a moment the two gazed at each other. Then Will spoke.

"I do not know you, old man. Get you hence. Those white hairs ill become a fool and jester."

The few icy words were as pitiless as deserved. Falstaff's face went pale. He glanced around him for sympathy, but met none. Then, what attempted force had failed to do, Will's scorn accomplished. Slowly, without a word, he crept to the door and left the theatre. What became of him I know not. He was not seen in London again.

There was an instant's silence after his exit. Then Robin Greene moved to follow him; but ere he had reached the door Will called to him.

"Come hither, Robin."

He turned, his thin face flushing with surprise. Will's voice was gentle.

"There is no place here for traitors; but thy enmity was open. Dost wish to be friends again?"

The lad was very young, and very feeble now, from hardships and hunger. The few kind, unexpected words unstrung him utterly. He cast himself at Will's feet and clung to his hand, weeping like a child. The other actors moved away, myself included, but we could hear Will's deep voice.

"There, cheer thee, lad, all is forgiven. What! I know that thy jealousy and anger drove thee mad, and that Jack Falstaff——"

"He said he hated thee in his heart," sobbed Robin, "and between us we made Marlowe drunk, and oh, Will, we might have killed thee;" and he fell to kissing the kindly hand to which he clung.

"But ye did not—and to-day we play at the palace. Come, lad, cheer thee and be one of us again."

And so, coaxing, consoling, he at last brought Robin Greene over to the rest of the players, red-eyed and ashamed, and ordered one of the minor actors to take him off to dinner and meet us later at the palace.

And then, with all his heart, he threw himself into the work of getting our costumes and properties in shape for temporary removal. I walked in a kind of happy dream, and the other actors seemed in tune with my mood. All were in high glee at the honor bestowed upon Will and upon the company, and I was as joyous as the rest for that reason and another. Finally, with jests and laughter, we left the theatre, and with neither mishap nor adventure reached the palace in good time.

All London knew that, after the Queen had eaten her Michaelmas goose, the players were to entertain her, and a large crowd had assembled in front of the palace to welcome us. They shouted good-natured jests at us, and the players returned their compliments

with interest. In the palace, too, as we passed through the various halls and apartments, we caused much excitement and delight, although in gentler wise. Once or twice I recognized a nobleman whom I had seen at the Globe. The ladies' faces were all strange to me; for no woman who valued her good name attended the theatre. At last we entered the long hall in which the play was to be given. Platform and curtains were already there, and it was deserted, by the Queen's orders, that we might make our preparations in peace. Finally, after a busy half-hour, all arrangements were completed, and word was sent to her Majesty that her poor players stood ready to do her bidding.

Then, indeed, for the first time I felt an instant's panic. Was I truly to look upon her glorious face, that Queen of whom poets sung, before whom sages trembled, at whose feet all men bowed in homage? Then, suddenly, my agitation was stilled as quickly as it had arisen. Will's comforting hand clasped mine.

"Courage, Cesario!" he exclaimed, aloud. "Thou hast less cause for fear than any of us, thou'st played thy part so well!"

His bright, tender smile, the double meaning in his words, his furtive caress, calmed me and gave me

251

confidence again. For his sake I could command myself. I smiled at him and lifted my head.

My courage had returned just in time. We heard voices without, heralding the approach of the Queen. An instant later the heavy doors were flung wide, and through them swept a glittering throng of courtiers. The players peeped through the curtains and beheld the gay multitude take their places. The costumes of both men and women were gorgeous, the jewels magnificent. So noble an array of handsome men and beauteous women I had never seen before, nor ever would again. Will, standing by my side, named some of them to me in a whisper. Yonder was Sir Philip Sidney, England's ideal. There was Sir Walter Raleigh, gentleman, adventurer, and friend of Edmund Spenser, the poet, now in Ireland. Beside him stood the Earl of Essex, fiery and impetuous, whom rumor said the Queen loved well. There was Leicester, too, another who sought her smiles, and Burleigh, pompous and self-contained. That slender lad was young Francis Bacon. He scorned plays and players, but came hither from policy because her Majesty loved them. That fair lady was the Countess of Pembroke, Sidney's sister; and yonder——

His whispered gossip came to an abrupt close. The courtiers, with one accord, bent low their heads. So did the players, though hidden by the curtains.

There was a cry of "Long live the Queen!" Then, through the midst of that glittering, obeisant crowd, she came, moving slow and stately. Her rich satin robe surpassed the numerous magnificent gowns around her. Her many jewels flashed a little world of light. She held high her haughty, warm-hued head, and walked with conscious grace.

So she came, through the light and the color and the homage that she loved, and reached, at length, her place; stood there an instant, then sank into the carved chair that awaited her. The court also seated themselves about and behind her. So she sat, imperious and brilliant, the slender woman who held all England in the strong white hand that lay idly on the chair-arm, the sovereign and mistress of many loyal hearts, Elizabeth, our Virgin Queen.

A courtier said something to her as she seated herself. I did not catch his words, nor the reply, but it must have been a sharp one, for he looked much discomfited. A page tittered at his expression, and her Majesty rewarded the saucy imp with a sharp box on

the ear; then turned her bright, piercing eyes on Will, as he stepped forward to speak the prologue.

"Thy name, Master Player," she called out suddenly, as he made his bow at its conclusion and was about to retire.

Will told her, bending his knee.

"Will Shakespeare," she repeated. "Rise, Will. 'Tis my will that thou shouldst do so." She smiled at the courtiers around her, and they laughed dutifully. "Proceed with thy play, Will, and if I will that the play please me, perchance 'twill be my will to take thee and thy companions under my protection."

"Ah, your Majesty——" began Will, assuming an expression of ecstatic delight.

"Proceed, Sir Player. The Court waits," she crisply cut him short.

The combat between the rival Montagues and Capulets and the succeeding scene followed. When it ended we heard sounds of applause, led by the Queen, and the soft, silvery comment of women's tongues rising above the deeper accents of the men. That pretty murmur was strange to me, accustomed to the entirely male audiences at the Globe, always as rough in their manifestations of approval as of disapproval.

The play, so auspiciously begun, continued smoothly, rapidly. I have had sadness in my life, but also many happy days, thank God. Methinks, when I say so, I thank Him both for the sorrow and the joy. And of all the glad remembrances I have locked within my memory, there is none more delightsome than that afternoon at the palace, when, my sex unknown, I played a double part before the Queen and the Court. And those love scenes with Will, formerly such torture, what delight were they now! The later ones of pain and death alone were not ours. It seemed, that bright day, that they could never be. And yet, if so——

> "Let love devouring death do what he dare,
>   It is enough I may but call her mine."

So Will, as Romeus, cried with passion, thinking of me, I knew, and in my heart the words devoutly were echoed.

The duel scene was difficult for us all. I was not on the stage, but, standing at the side, I saw on Marlowe's brow great drops of sweat, quite unwarranted by his exertions. Robin Greene, beside me, for he had no part in the play, of course, groaned and hid his face in his hands. Marlowe, indeed, fenced so care-

fully that he had to be urged to put more spirit into the duel, that it might not seem a farce.

At length, however, the trying scene was safely concluded, and there began the entirely new part of the play, the scenes which had never been given in public, owing to the untimely ending of that first performance.

The Queen had been watching me with special intentness from the beginning. The other actors noticed and commented upon this fact, and offered me laughing, although sincere, congratulations. Her steady gaze made me slightly uncomfortable, for my part was no more important than Will's, yet she did not look at him so constantly. When, at length, Juliet drank the Friar's potion, I was alone upon the stage, and just as I lifted the phial to my lips the Queen's intent gaze met mine again. I stammered a little over my part, in sheer embarrassment, and almost dropped the tiny bottle.

The play drew near its close. Juliet lay sleeping in her death-like trance, and Romeus came to take his last farewell. In the corpse-like rigidity of my attitude I could not see the audience, but I felt the Queen's bright, steady eyes still upon me. A few moments

later, while I searched for Romeus's dagger, I noted that her gaze yet intently followed all my actions.

Romeus and Juliet, the star-crossed lovers, lay at rest. The play was ended. The curtains were drawn together. In the babel of applause and conversation that followed we heard the Queen's voice speaking distinctly.

"Where is Will Shakespeare? Where is Romeus?"

Obeying the summons, Will passed out between the curtains and stood before her. The rest of us peeped, and saw her gazing at his noble figure critically.

"A fine play, Will Shakespeare," she said at length. "Thou shalt act others here, and often, if they prove so good as this. Where is thy Juliet?"

Will came back for me, and I followed him, trembling. We stood together before her. The jewels sparkled bright upon her person, but her eyes outshone them in hardness and brilliancy. Methought I should not care to have those eyes turned on me in anger. Yet withal, there was a certain graciousness about her, an air of majesty and charm which made me dimly understand at that moment why she could draw such men and women around her. I knew, now, why she

257

had excited tributes of loyalty and devotion so passionate from men whom no bribes could have forced to adulation. She gazed at us both an instant with that bright, penetrating gaze; then nodded to a courtier.

"Clear the room," she said, imperiously.

"Your Majesty?" the nobleman faltered, thinking he misunderstood.

"Clear the room," she repeated, "of all, of courtiers and players alike. I would speak to Romeus and Juliet alone."

In a few moments her command was obeyed. The long, stately apartment was empty save for us three. The Queen sat there, looking at me as she had done in the play. I trembled, wondering what her steady gaze meant. I never dreamed of the truth. At length she spoke.

"What means this? A maid disguised as a man among players?"

With a surprised exclamation I was bathed in blushes as in a flame. I stood there, my head drooping. Will gave a low, amused laugh, and put his arm around me.

"We might have known it was impossible to de-

258

ceive your Majesty," he said, tactfully, holding me close the while. "I am the only player who knows Juliet's sex. Your Majesty's eyes are keen."

"But why is this?" the Queen persisted, although her face relaxed somewhat at Will's subtle flattery. " 'Tis a scandal, were it known, Master Player."

"Nay, then," replied Will, readily; "you shall have the tale, your Majesty, an it please you to listen. You will find it another play, indeed."

Then, briefly, softly, eloquently, he narrated our love-story as I have striven to write it here; but ah! how infinitely more touching and tender it was on his lips! 'Twas a tale, as he told it, to melt any woman's heart.

When at last he had finished, the Queen sat gazing at him with a look of wonder and admiration. Methought there were even tears in her bright eyes.

"A tale fit for a play, indeed," she said, and she sighed a little; "a tale fit for a play, indeed."

She paused a moment. Then she added, more impulsively than I yet had heard her speak:

"I am glad to know thee, Master Shakespeare, and thee, also, madam," courteously to me. Then, more calmly, "What dost intend to do with thy sweetheart,

Master Shakespeare? The theatre is no place for a woman."

"We return to Stratford to-morrow," I heard Will answer, to my surprise. "I shall come back to London as speedily as may be, and I hope for a continuance of the favor your Majesty hath shown me to-day."

She smiled suddenly, graciously, and gave him her hand to kiss.

"Thou hast it, sir," she said, "thou hast it, e'en— well, e'en for the sake of thy brave sweetheart, and the tale that thou hast told so well. Ay, Will Shakespeare, thou shalt be under my patronage henceforth, and thy fortunes shall be my care."

She interrupted herself, still smiling:

"Nay," she said, graciously, "thy fortune is already thine; for this thy sweetheart is treasure rich enough."

She bent forward, in stately fashion, and kissed me on the mouth.

"There, Mistress Shakespeare," she went on, "thou canst say until thy dying day that thou bearest a Queen's kiss upon thy lips. Go back to Stratford with thy husband and let thy trust in him henceforth be perfect. Such as he grow not on every bush. As for thee, Will Shakespeare, shame consume thee if thou

dost ever play her false! Soothly, methinks ye have proved to the full each other's love and truth. Nay, thank me no thanks. The play is well ended. Call in the Court, Master Shakespeare."

Chapter XIX

After Life's Fit-ful Fever

The next day, as Will had told the Queen, we started back to Stratford, thereby creating much wonderment among the players. Master Jonson and Master Burbadge urged Will strongly not to leave London just after his success at the palace. He stood in his own light by so doing, they said. But Will was firm. He could not explain to them why he felt so sure of a continuance of her Majesty's favor, nor make them understand why he was so suddenly seized with a desire to visit Stratford. Cesario, he said, he would take with him, because the lad had come from Stratford, and was homesick. It remained unknown that I was not to return to London.

Ah, what a happy journey it was that we made together, comrade-wise, from London to Stratford! When I had come to the great city it had been springtime. The birds had sung love-notes on every bush and tree. The tender flowers had been budding. All

things had told of youth and hope and sweetness; and yet my heart had been aged, and despairing, and bitter. Now it was autumn, and the leaves had begun to fall. The birds were hushed. The landscape spoke of change, and sorrow, and death; yet my spirit sang for joy within my bosom. True, change would come, and sorrow, also, and death; yet what mattered it when I had love immortal?

I kept my boy's disguise, for it was more convenient for the journey, and we would arrive at Stratford at nightfall. As we rode together through the beautiful autumn land it was as if the past months were blotted out. Once more we paced through Stratford roads to Charlcote, and talked eagerly of our love, of Will's aspirations. And now we had also our child to talk about and long for.

"Think, I have never seen her," Will said; "but thy letters made her live for me. I wondered much that none had come while I was ill, and had planned to go to Stratford when the play at the palace was safely over. Suppose I had not discovered thy sex, and that I had carried out my idea. What wouldst thou have done, Cesario?" His eyes twinkled as he used my assumed name.

266

"I know not," I answered, laughing, "but I would have found a way to deceive thee still, had I chosen. Trust woman's wit for that! No doubt the letters thou hast sent to Stratford since my departure are still unopened, since my grandam can neither read nor write. Poor grandam! Ah, Will, why is it? I am sorry now for the grief and anxiety she must have suffered; yet during all these months in London I have never thought of her. And the child—I love her dearly; and yet, when I made up my mind to come to thee, she seemed as naught, and I cared not what became of her. Why, Will, why?"

He shook his head, his calm and level gaze resting upon me, yet looking also beyond.

"Who knows?" he said. "Who knows? It was to be. 'Tis all we understand. And it was well that thou didst so. Let us thank God."

A moment later he spoke of the Countess.

"She has left London," he said. "She went while we were at the palace. I heard it this morning from Count William, who came to bid me farewell. He hath followed her, and will go to the ends of the earth to comfort and to succor her."

I thought of her with pity and with sorrow, and

267

breathed a prayer for her and for the Count. Then I looked once more on my dear love, and suddenly a great wave of remorse rushed over me for my past lack of faith in him, so noble and so true. I stretched my hands towards him beseechingly.

"Forgive," I whispered. "Forgive——"

He gave me one great, tender glance of love and comprehension; then took both my hands in his, and bent and kissed them with gentle reverence.

"Sweetheart!" he said. "Sweetheart!"

When at last we arrived in Shottery, tired and travel-stained, we found a hearty welcome. How my babe laughed and lisped childish words of joy at sight of me, and smiled at her father, as if she had known him all her life! How my grandam wept with delight to see us both together again, and in happiness! How we jested over my disguise, and what trouble I had to remove the dye from my hair, the stain from my face and hands! At length it was agreed that I should not appear in public for a few days, so that both might have time to wear off. Meanwhile my grandam was to announce among the gossips that I had returned, quite recovered, from the place whither she had sent me to heal my wandering wits.

268

Ay, that was a happy journey, a blessed home-coming. And, thank God, it was but the beginning of many happy and blessed years.

The rest of our love-story is so peaceful and joyous that it can be told in a short space. 'Tis well that this is so; for I fear me my chronicle hath already spread beyond the limits that Master Jonson planned.

I am an old woman now, and I can look back and say that the bliss that God hath granted me hath far outweighed the bitterness that He saw fit also to send. My shadowed girlhood, and those weary months when I deemed Will false to me, were difficult, indeed, to bear; but against them are set many happy years of sunshine, and prosperity, and loyal love. The joy that entered my life when Will first came into it was eclipsed for a time, but it returned, a brighter light than ever, to shine steadily, beneficently, unto the end.

We had our sorrows. Will's family never approved of me, and his mother refused always to look upon me as a daughter. Will was a dutiful son, but after that night at Charlcote he was scarce a loving one. When at length she died, he attended her funeral as an outsider. To his father he brought a renewal of fortune, as his fame grew in London.

269

In the course of time my grandam died, also; a woman with whom life had dealt hardly, but who received, I dare to hope, some compensation from my perfect happiness. Will wept at her grave, as he had not at his mother's.

Other children besides Susannah came to us; twins, Hamnet and Judith. Hamnet lived a few brief, bright, boyish years, then passed to the Beyond. He was such a child as his father must have been; and had he lived, perhaps—perhaps—but I will not awaken an old sorrow. In his innocence he went home to God. What more dare I desire? Sometimes, during these latter days, since Will has left me, I have thought what joy it would be had I a son to lean upon—a son with his father's eyes, as Hamnet had. But God knows best. If my checkered life has taught me nothing else, it has taught me this. 'Tis an old lesson, but passing difficult to learn.

There was much lamentation when Will first went back to London without Cesario, and many inquiries as to why and wherefore he had left me. Will replied, with truth, that Cesario had been so well pleased to reach home again that he had no desire to return to London, and, moreover, that he was married. At the

270

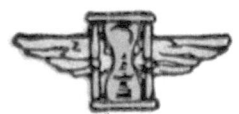

last news the players raised a great shout of laughter, remembering my boyish appearance, and they sent their congratulations to me by Will when next he came to Stratford.

The Queen kept her promise and gave Will's company her patronage. He became steadily more prosperous. I am glad to think that his genius alone would have brought him fame in time; but the Queen's gracious favor made his pathway smooth.

Several times her Majesty summoned him to a secret audience and inquired after my well-being. Once or twice she sent me a message, royal and gracious. No hint of my disguise ever reached either London or Stratford. Strangely, almost unexpectedly, the secret was well kept.

But once in all those years we heard of the Count and Countess. I know not now whether they still live; or, if they are dead, what was their fate. A letter came once to Will, several years after my return to Stratford; a letter written from some sunny, retired spot in Italy. It ran as follows, without heading or signature:

"I am with her. 'Tis enough. She is changed, gentler and more tender; also, alas! more frail. I fear

271

me she is not long for the earth. She bids me give you both her blessing and farewell.

"'That blessing comes from wicked lips,' she added; 'but—but the lips of St. Mary the Magdalen—were they not sacred after they had touched the feet of our Lord? And I, weak and sinful, lie in the dust before Him. Therefore, perhaps, e'en my benediction——' and with that she sighed, and would say no more.

"We are not wedded. She would not have it so. As a brother am I to her, ministering to her wants. I come to see her each day, and each day she seems nearer death. Thou, Will, who seest not as other men, and thy sweetheart wife, who is above all women, save one, in my thought—you will understand that there is no sin in our relations now, nor ever was between us two. Pray for us, and farewell."

So abruptly the letter ended, and we never received another. When those two, one scarlet-robed and crowned with dusky tresses, the other golden-haired and clad in blue the color of the sky—when they passed from our sight that day before Paul's, they also went out of our lives forever.

As the years went on and Will's prosperity grew,

272

however, I again saw other faces which had grown dear to me in London. Will bought New Place and established his family therein. Thus I came, an honored and wealthy matron, into the town where, as a nameless child, I had been glanced at askance, and served in menial wise. Mistress Quickly rejoiced over my rise in the world, and fussed over the children to her heart's content. Good, homely friend, God bless her!

Many of Will's comrades, after he had a home of his own, were invited to enjoy his hospitality, and so I met again stately Burbadge, and comical Kempe, kindly Jonson, and reckless Marlowe, young Greene and all the rest. Not one of them, however, ever recognized Cesario, the page, in Anne Shakespeare, the matron. The first time any came I trembled lest they should do so; but my fears were groundless. Several years had passed. My hair was once more golden and my skin fair. Moreover, none suspected the truth. Once or twice some of them asked Will if he ever saw Cesario, and he always replied, solemnly, that he thought the lad must have moved to another part of the country, since he had disappeared so entirely; and this ended the matter.

My daughters grew up and were wedded; first Susannah, then Judith. The latter, Will's favorite, was married shortly before his death, and he took much pleasure in arranging the details of the ceremony. She was a saucy wench, with yellow hair and sparkling blue eyes; and he delighted in teasing her and listening to her apt replies. Ah, well, both she and Sue are good girls and made happy marriages. Their joy in their husbands and their households gladdens me whenever I visit them.

Although I still live in the body, my true life ended five years ago, or, rather, waits for me in Paradise. For, as I said in the beginning, it is five years since he left us and the world that loves and mourns him still. His end was untimely, for he was in vigorous health, apparently, and it seemed as if he would live many years. One day he was laughing and jesting with some of his London friends as they supped together in the garden. The next he lay in mortal illness.

The disease, whatever it may have been, was speedy in its course. He soon sank into a stupor whence naught could rouse him save my voice. He knew me and responded to my call until the end—

274

which came all too rapidly, a few days after he was stricken.

It was midnight and I was alone with him. The house was very still. I felt that death was near. My eyes were fixed on his face in passionate entreaty, my hand was clasped in his. Suddenly he awoke, and knew me, for he smiled. Then his gaze left my face and rested on the starlit world without.

'Twas a perfect spring night. The full moon rode glorious in the heavens. The stars were a vast multitude about her. The murmur of the Avon sounded full and clear. So he lay an instant, drinking in with his dying senses the beauty of the world that he had loved so well. Then, quite clearly and distinctly, ere his eyes closed for the last time, he spoke——

"Forever!" he said; and then again, more faintly, "Forever! Forever!"

But whether he spoke of our undying love, or of the immortal beauty of the world, or of that strange new Life and Love that he was fast approaching—who shall say?

His London comrades and his Stratford friends came to the funeral, and he was buried with much honor in the chancel of our little church. There was

sore weeping and heartfelt grief; for all who knew him loved him right well. As I stood beside his burial place I realized that all my heart was there; and that, although my body might live on many years, my soul was in communion with his eternally henceforth in the Beyond.

So there, in the quiet Stratford church by the river, he lies, and there he will rest forever. No rude, un-hallowed hand will seek to disturb his helpless dust, and so invoke the curse he has called down in his epitaph on any who dares remove his bones from that quiet resting-place. As some saint's relic, that hal-lowed dust makes Stratford sacred; and many pilgrims will travel hither to do him honor in the years to come.

And for me—I am not and cannot be altogether desolate. My daughters are married and away, but they come often and are dutiful girls. Yet it is not their presence that keeps me from loneliness. 'Tis rather the voices of the wind and the river, which speak of him constantly to me. It is the glory of the moon and the stars in midnight majesty which makes live for me once more that mysterious last hour of his upon earth. It is the tranquil twilight when, sitting

alone, I were not surprised to see him rise from among the shadows. Ah, no, I am not lonely! He is always very near. Loving me in life, he could not, even in death, desert me. Such is my Credo and my comfort.

My chronicle is ended. There are many things in it that will greatly surprise Master Jonson. Perhaps, when he has finished it, he will think best that it be not published. That is as he pleases. It matters not to me. I have finished the task he set me, and now I may rest.

Rest grows very sweet as life draws near its close. Ah, eternal rest, when wilt thou come to me? Empty world, when shall I leave thee? Will's last words have been echoing often in my mind of late. Oh, hasten, blessed time, when I shall have my heart's desire and see his face again; when love and life both shall be mine—forever!

Master Jonson's Epilogue

Mistress Shakespeare's revelation is a great surprise to me, as she anticipated. None of us ever dreamed that Cesario was aught else than he appeared. We regretted his untimely departure, and often said that he had played his part as if he were indeed a woman. We meant it for idle compliment. Behold, it was true!

Methought Mistress Shakespeare's chronicle would be a few brief pages; and see its bulk! Verily, women's ways are strange. She hath poured out her very heart in this volume, careless who shall behold it. Shall I, for Will's sake, for her sake, make it public?

I cannot, alas! consult with her about it, nor advise alterations and omissions. A week or two ago, shortly after she had finished this history, she died, quite suddenly and painlessly, Will's name upon her lips. She had had many trials, yet she was a happy woman. Will Shakespeare's wife could not be otherwise. I shall not soon forget the smile of perfect joy

281

and peace that rested on her dead face when her body lay prepared for burial.

None knows of the existence of this manuscript save myself. Shall I destroy it, or——

Soothly, I will leave it for time to decide. The problem is too great for me to solve. In the cellar of the Mermaid there is a secret underground vault. Few know of its existence. In an obscure corner there, in an air-tight box, I will deposit this chronicle. Then, if it ever be discovered, well. If not, let it moulder in obscurity. Time shall decide.

They are together again. None can wish them greater happiness, not even I, who loved them right well. Rest peacefully, thou Star of Poets, and thou Star of Women. The world will never know your like. Some day, perhaps, I shall meet ye both again. Towards that hope my spirit yearns. Meanwhile the world is dark without you. Until we meet again, farewell, Will, dear comrade and poet; farewell, Anne Hathaway, Shakespeare's Sweetheart.

www.ingramcontent.com/pod-product-compliance
Lightning Source LLC
Chambersburg PA
CBHW020603260626
47157CB00003B/851